SECRET COOKIES

Cookie Corner Mysteries
Book Nine

CINDY STARK

www.cindystark.com

ONE

September sun painted Honeysuckle Spring's city park with a soft golden stroke that lazy Sunday afternoon. Caden, Kookie, and I had been there for a while, but I was unwilling to call it a day even though there weren't many daylight hours left.

I sat there, cross-legged on the lush grass, watching Caden and Kookie with a heart full of mixed emotions from newfound joys and untold secrets as I thought about my life. The sun's rays caught the surface of the engagement ring resting on my hand, the feel of the band around my finger still noticeably new.

The moment Caden had proposed filled me with incredible happiness, along with a heightened state of worry. I *had* to tell him how my Aunt Birdie now lived in her familiar Theo's body. But I feared my unwillingness to have already confessed the secret would feel like a betrayal to him.

Still, I couldn't put it off much longer or it would make things even worse. But with Chloe's wedding only weeks away, her exciting preparations occupied much of my attention. Or maybe I was just stalling. But I decided I'd focus on her for the time being, promising myself I'd find a way to tell Caden before that day arrived.

My handsome police chief was sprawled out next to me, his laughter low and easy as he observed Kookie chasing shadows caused by a breeze blowing through the remaining leaves on the trees. The sun cast highlights on his dark hair, and his stormy gray eyes twinkled with delight. "Such a curious little girl."

And pretty, Kookie added, her thoughts invading mine along with the vibrations of her purrs as she stalked the dancing spots on the grass.

I chuckled at her antics and pushed aside my worries, not wanting to spoil the beautiful moment. "There's a whole world of mischief inside her."

I leaned forward, my fingers grazing the tabby's soft orange and black fur. The contented rumble from her tiny chest floated toward me, chasing away my remaining worries. There was so much love between the three of us at that moment that I knew everything would be okay.

As Kookie sauntered closer to Caden, demanding his attention with a nudge of her head, I let the serenity of the moment wash over me. I soaked in the scent of dried leaves hanging heavy in the air, kissed with a chill, promising colder months weren't far away. Which was part of the reason I'd wanted to get out and enjoy the day.

I watched Caden with Kookie, his hands gentle, his smile soft. He was my love, the one I'd share years and years with, and suddenly, my fears crept back in. My thoughts took flight, imagining how he would react to knowing his future aunt-in-law was currently enjoying her life in feline form.

There was only one way to find out, but I didn't relish it. If I was honest with myself, there would never be a good time to tell him, and perhaps postponing the inevitable would only make things worse.

Seize the day.

The words echoed in my head, and I wondered if it was a message of warning from the Goddess. One that I should listen to. I inhaled a deep breath, deciding to spill the truth, when the sharp trill of his phone sliced through the quiet and squelched my wavering confession.

As he listened to the caller, the lines of his face hardened, and his body stiffened into the stance of Police Chief Bexley, the man who safeguarded the peace of Honeysuckle Springs. He scrubbed his chin as he listened, worry furrowing his brows, and he ended the call by saying, "I'll be right there."

Just like that, our beautiful day vanished, and the park, once a haven, now felt like the edge of an abyss. I spoke, my voice barely above a whisper, afraid to ask what news he'd received. "Something's happened. What is it?"

He pocketed his phone and met my gaze, his eyes a storm about to break. "There's been a murder."

The weight of those words crushed the last bit of tranquility that had lingered in the air as he stood and held out a hand to me. Kookie's ears pricked up, and she leapt onto my shoulder, a warm, solid presence. I held her with one hand and grasped him with the other, letting him pull me up.

"Oh, Goddess, no. *Who? Where?*"

Caden turned, his steps purposeful as he headed toward the parking lot, tugging me along with him. Kookie's weight on my shoulder comforted me as much as I reassured her.

He met my gaze with worried eyes. "Nan Collingsworth."

The moisture in my mouth evaporated. "Nan?" The woman creating Chloe's wedding dress?

A surge of worry for my best friend mingled with my shock. How would this affect her, since she was already stressed with wedding plans? And poor Nan. She'd lost her life? The possible consequences for my friend could wait, but there was no denying the two were fatefully intertwined.

Caden halted at the passenger side of his truck and pulled open the door. "I'll drive you home and grab my work car while I'm there."

I placed Kookie on the seat and peered at him, feeling guilty that I was still using his truck as my main transportation since the disaster with my car. "Don't waste time. Just take me with you, and I'll find a way home."

He paused with his hand on the door. He narrowed his gaze, and I was certain he could see right through me. "It's a murder investigation, Evie. You can't be in the middle of it, and the scene might be dangerous."

I cut him off. "I won't get in the way. I promise. But Chloe's my best friend, and Nan was making her dress. I need to know what happened so I can help her."

Caden studied me for a moment, then nodded once. "Okay. But you stay in the truck until your ride arrives, unless I say otherwise."

I agreed, knowing this was the only concession I'd get. I climbed into the passenger seat, and he closed the door between us. A moment later, he was behind the wheel, and we were off.

The drive to Nanette's Creations was a blur of pine trees and glimpses of Skipper Lake, the hallmark of our Northern Idaho lakeside town. The silence was interspersed with Kookie's soft breathing next to my ear, and I knew she sensed the gravity of the situation.

When we arrived at the shop in the center of town, the scene was chaos held at bay by yellow tape and flashing lights. Caden was out of the truck in an instant. He moved with a speed that was all business, all chief of police. I watched him, this man I was going to marry, and felt a twinge of pride mixed with a dash of fear. His dedication was one of the things I loved about him, but in moments like this, it also meant he was stepping into harm's way.

Through the truck window, I could see the soft rose exterior of Nan's shop, now a crime scene. I pushed aside thoughts of Chloe, of how this would affect her, and leaned forward, trying to catch a glimpse of anything that might tell me more.

When that proved fruitless, I groaned and reached for the door handle. "We can't see anything from here."

Kookie admonished me with a chuff. *Caden said to stay in the truck, and you said you would.*

I chuckled softly over her worries. "That's because he thought it would be dangerous. But as you can see, it's not. The police are everywhere. Obviously, we can't go inside, but that doesn't mean we can't sneak closer for a better look."

She eyed me with uncertainty, as though the rules of my world confused her. *But when you tell me to stay put, you get mad when I don't.*

I tugged her from my shoulder and held her tightly against me, thinking how easily I'd offered that white lie to Caden. Although at the time I'd said it, I'd meant it. Mostly. "That's different. You're only a kitten. I'm more experienced in the world and capable of making adult decisions."

As I stepped out, she tilted her cute little head, still eyeing me with suspicion.

Nothing stood between us and the building housing Nanette's Creations, other than a few pots of chrysanthemums and slender pines. I moved as close as I possibly could and peered in through the large picture window. Mannequins dressed in formal wear blocked much of my view along with several officers working the scene, but after a moment, I saw *it*.

Through the shifting people and the glare of the lights, I caught sight of Nan's body on the floor. The mid-portion of her, to be exact. The rest remained out of sight. The white fabric she wore was stained with something too dark to be anything but blood, and a pair of glinting shears protruded from her chest.

I sucked in a shocked breath as sadness from the loss of her life overwhelmed me. That was until I noticed the details of the bodice and choked. Clasping my throat, I blinked and looked harder. But there was no mistaking the swirls of seed pearls and ivory lace.

What is it?

Kookie's thoughts snapped me back to my senses. I stepped away as the implications spun in my head, a tangle of fear and confusion, and I focused on my kitten. "This is worse than I thought, Kookie." I lowered my voice to a whisper. *"Nan was murdered while wearing Chloe's dress."*

Kookie blinked twice, her peculiar yellow eyes widening each time, and her thoughts brushed against mine. *This is really bad.*

When Caden appeared on the other side of the glass, blocking my view, I startled. He chastised me with a fierce look, jabbed a finger in my direction, and then did the same toward his truck. Then he arched his brows, visually asking if I understood, and I tucked my lips inward, sending him a look of apology before I turned away.

I hadn't called anyone to pick us up, and I didn't intend to until I'd learned what I could, but I didn't want to worry Caden, either.

He watched us until we were back in the truck before returning to his work. I stayed where I'd promised I would, but my mind was already inside the shop, searching for clues, trying to make sense of a senseless act.

Somewhere in the back of my mind, a thought took hold. This wasn't just a murder. *This was personal.* Likely not premeditated since the murderer had used Nan's shears, but to stab her with her own tools made a significant statement.

Nan had angered someone to the point of seeing red. But who? And why?

Two

Early evening had closed in by the time Caden emerged from Nan's shop. The day's worries etched his face and tugged at my heart. I hoped Honeysuckle Springs appreciated how dedicated he was to his job.

Chloe's fiancé, Officer Riley Weaver, with his sandy blond hair and big shoulders, was close behind him. The two men approached with a somber air, their shadows long in the flashing lights of the squad cars. Caden opened my door and gazed at me with a disappointed look. "I thought you were calling someone to pick you up."

I lifted my shoulders in a guilty shrug. "I was going to. I promise. Initially, I'd thought to call Chloe, but then decided being here might not be good for her."

Riley nodded, concern for his bride in his hazel eyes. "Yeah, I agree. If Nan hasn't finished her dress, it'll really throw a wrench in her wedding plans."

Caden arched his brow. "Assuming she'd still want to wear it. Chloe might see it as a bad omen, wearing a dress that witnessed the murder of its creator."

A lump formed in my throat, hating to tell them the reality was way worse than what they knew. "There's more. It's not just that Nan made her dress." I covered my mouth for a long moment, steeling myself. "Nan's *wearing* it right now. This isn't just a delay. *It's a disaster.*"

Riley's face paled, and he shoved a hand through his hair. "Oh, gads. Chloe's going to be frantic. She's been on edge about every detail, and now this…"

He looked at me, his gaze pleading. "Evie, I need to be here, but she's going to need someone. Soon. Before anyone else can tell her. I hate to ask, but can I put this on you?"

I nodded, feeling the weight of his request. Not that he needed to ask. I'd always be there for my best friend. Poor Chloe, with her heart set on the perfect wedding, was now faced with her dreams being snatched away so cruelly. It was more than just a dress. It was the symbol of her new beginning, now stained with tragedy.

I steadied my voice despite the turmoil inside. "Of course, Riley. I'll take care of her. You need to focus on work."

Caden lifted his chin at me. "Take the truck. I'll catch a ride when we're done."

I nodded my thanks. "I'll call Chloe right now before the rumor spreads."

Both gave me grateful nods and turned back to the crime scene, leaving me to break the hardest news. I phoned Chloe, my gut twisting. When she answered, her voice was bright, a stark contrast to the darkness around me. "Hey, Evie. I can't talk long, Riley and I—"

"I know," I said, cutting in, forcing a lightness into my tone that I didn't feel. "Actually, that's why I'm calling. Police duties have stolen both our guys. How about dinner? Just us girls."

There was a pause, and I could almost hear Chloe's mind working, rearranging her plans. "Oh, well, sure. I guess that'll be okay. What's going on? Riley hasn't called to let me know."

I took a deep breath, my heart aching for her. "Some unexpected police stuff, and I told him I'd let you know. I'll tell you more when I see you. Will you be ready in about thirty minutes?" That would give me enough time to get home, drop off Kookie, and compose myself.

A hint of disappointment colored her voice. "Yeah. Sounds good. See you soon."

Discontent would be the least of her worries before long, and I wished I could let her bask in her innocence for a while longer. But the rumor mill in our little town ran at lightning speed. As soon as nosey realtor Miranda found out, she'd surely call a bunch of people, including Chloe's mom Valerie. If the news spread before I got to Chloe, I'd be lucky if Valerie was the one who'd tell her. But I couldn't take that chance.

A half-hour later, my headlights cut through the shadows, silhouetting the new townhouse Chloe shared with Riley. I spotted my best friend waiting on the porch, huddled into her bright yellow puffer jacket. Her blond hair glowed under the bright light, and she stood as I pulled to the side of the road.

She climbed into the passenger seat of Caden's truck, and a waft of her floral perfume mixed with the evening air, leaving me with a scent that was distinctly Chloe. Gentle and unassuming. She clicked her seatbelt in place and greeted me with a smile. "I guess this all worked out for the best anyway. I've been wanting a girl's night before the wedding, and now you can help me go over all the final details."

As if we hadn't already done the same several times. But I'd never been a bride, so I could only guess how anxious I'd be under the same circumstances. I forced a smile. "I'm here for whatever you need."

The warmth in her expression deepened the worry in my heart. As I pulled away from the curb, I steeled my emotions to prepare for my coming disclosure. Chloe loved to chat mindlessly anyway, so I let her steer the conversation as I drove to the Gooseberry Café.

Lights from the restaurant alongside the highway at the edge of town shined like beacons as we approached. The café's windows were aglow, illuminating the raised flower beds that lined the walkway. The rustic charm of the place was a balm to the soul.

I parked, and we stepped out of the truck. The scent of the earth after a day warmed by the sun reached us, grounding and real. The café's door chimed our arrival, a sound that usually brought a sense of comfort. Tonight, it was the prelude to a difficult revelation.

Inside, various conversations blended into one, and the rich aroma of roasted beans tickled my senses. The interior was a cocoon of earthy tones and textures, the handcrafted items adorning the walls and the artisanal ceramics a testament to the town's blend of the modern and mystical.

I led the way to a booth at the back of the café and chose the seat facing the other patrons. I hadn't considered imparting difficult news to Chloe in a public place might not have been a smart move, but it was too late to change now. So, I'd offer her as much privacy as our setting would allow.

Chloe slid into the booth across from me and grabbed a menu, opening it with interest. "Now that we're here, I'm starving."

I groaned internally. Did I let her enjoy the meal before telling her? Or risk upsetting her stomach if I waited until afterward?

If it was me, I supposed I'd rather hear the news straightaway. I waited for the server to take our orders and bring drinks before I focused on Chloe with a serious look. "You asked what Caden and Riley were up to."

She nodded as she sipped her soda, her gaze drifting out the large window to the side of our booth. But before I could respond, she choked on a swallow, her eyes watering. "Oh, my God."

My mind struggled to shift gears as I followed her gaze through the glass. A guy with shaggy brown hair, a touch too long, slowed as he strolled past, his intense gaze focused on Chloe. I glanced at her in time to see her lift a hesitant hand in greeting, her lips curving into a surprised smile.

The man responded with a wide grin, his eyes brightening as he waved in return. Once he passed our window, the smile fell from my friend's face, and she turned to me with a concerned look. "This is not good. Not good at all."

I jerked my gaze from her and craned my neck to look back at the guy who was obviously intent on entering the restaurant. "Who's that?"

She dropped her face into her hand momentarily. "A ghost from the past. Brandon Simmons. He lived in a nearby town, and we dated seriously a few years ago."

I arched my brows in surprise as a slow smile curved my lips. "Oh, really? He seemed happy to see you."

Her breath eased out of her as she slowly shook her head. "Don't say that."

My thoughts of teasing faded. "Why not? Was it a bad breakup?"

She shrugged. "We didn't exactly break up. He went away to college, and it just sort of fizzled from there. He kept drifting farther away, all while promising me I meant everything to him." She huffed a breath. "I'd just prefer to never see him again."

Seconds after Chloe finished her sentence, Brandon approached our table, and I tried to warn my friend by widening my eyes and tilting my head.

Brandon's gaze met mine for a brief second before he spoke. "Chloe."

She turned in her seat, her kind smile back in place. "Brandon. Wow. I never thought I'd see you again."

THREE

Chloe's smile remained on her face while she spoke to her former love, Brandon, and I sensed the chill beneath her words. "It's been what, three years?"

He tossed the hair from his brow with a shake of his head, his hazel eyes seeming to carry the weight of past regrets. His jeans and a rumpled t-shirt spoke of a less structured life. "Yeah. I guess it's been about that. Too long. That's for sure."

Tension flickered in her gaze. "What brings you back to our neck of the woods?"

Brandon's gaze lingered on her, love still smoldering in his eyes, a flame not quite extinguished. "I've been back for a few months. Came home when my grandpa died and didn't return for the next semester. I've been taking classes online instead."

Chloe nodded. "I see."

Their exchange was a dance of awkwardness that skirted around the edges of what was and what could have been. I interrupted, hoping to help. "Hi, Brandon. I'm Evie, Chloe's friend."

He reluctantly shifted his gaze to me, an affable look hovering in his eyes. "It's nice to meet you, Evie. You must be new to town."

I supposed in a small town like Honeysuckle, my newness would be obvious. "I moved here a few months back after my great aunt died. You might have known her. Birdie St. Claire?"

Brandon released a soft huff. "Yeah, I knew her. She was a little crazy, but a lot of fun. I remember her getting carried away during a square dance a few years back."

His recollection brought a smile to my face. "That sounds like my Aunt Birdie. She had an unmatched zest for life." And still did. Though she now showed off her antics in a cat's body.

He shifted a look of longing back to Chloe, and I couldn't help but notice his gaze landing on my friend's engagement ring, the symbol of a future that didn't include him. "I guess I should've come back sooner," he said, the words hanging between them, heavy with unspoken meaning.

Chloe shrugged. "I guess life takes us where it takes us."

The moment stretched, increasing the uneasiness, until the server arrived with our burgers and fries. Brandon seemed to take the hint, and he thumbed over his shoulder. "Well, I'll let you two eat. Good seeing you, Chloe."

And just like that, he walked away, his departure a release of the tension we'd been holding. Chloe stared at me, unwilling to turn her gaze to follow him. "Tell me when it's safe."

I chuckled softly. "Depends on your version of safe. He's not leaving, but the table he claimed is near the entrance, away from us."

She dropped her shoulders. "Why me? Why now?"

I dunked a fry in ketchup, thinking of the news I still needed to deliver. "Life likes to throw curveballs. That's for sure."

A soft sigh escaped her as if she were releasing the remnants of a long-held memory. She turned back to me, a wistful smile curving her lips. "He was my first love. We were just kids when we met, but I thought we would end up together." She drew her finger through the condensation on her glass, a small gesture betraying her inner turmoil.

I dipped my head as I chewed, offering a silent encouragement for her to continue.

Slowly, her smile faded as she appeared to collect her thoughts. "But life had other plans. Brandon went off to college with all these big dreams, and like I said before, things slowly fell apart."

I nodded, hoping to comfort her. "That happens. Probably more often than not. Especially with first loves."

She shrugged, a delicate lift of her shoulders that seemed to carry the unwanted weight of her past. "I got over him, eventually. Found my own way. And then Riley came along, and everything just clicked."

As she bit into her hamburger and wiped her mouth, I recalled my first day in Honeysuckle Springs, and the interaction between Chloe and Riley. I smiled, thinking of her inability to recognize his interest back then. "Clicked in a big way, I'd say."

Some of her melancholy lifted. "Seeing Brandon now is strange. It's like looking through a window to a past that feels both close and yet so far away."

I tilted my head, sending her a determined look. "You've built a beautiful life, Chloe. One that's all your own. And Riley is a part of that. A *big* part. Obviously, you cared for Brandon back then, but from my perspective, you're no longer that girl."

A smile returned to her face, one that reached her eyes this time. "You're right. I'm happy with Riley. Truly happy. Brandon's a chapter that's already been written and closed." She snorted. "I just wish I hadn't run into him again."

Although the remnants of Brandon's presence still clung to the air as we ate, several minutes later, I knew the time had come to deliver the news that would go far beyond the ripple he'd created. But that couldn't be helped.

I swallowed my bite of burger and reached across the table, taking Chloe's hand in mine, my gesture a silent apology for the news I was about to deliver. Her hand was warm, a lifeline as I sought the right words to say.

Her eyes grew wide and expectant, searching mine for a hint of the conversation's direction. I steeled myself. "There's something I need to tell you. It's about the wedding…"

From the look on her face, I knew she'd clued into the seriousness of our topic, but she tried to shrug it off with a chuckle. "Stop, Evie. You're scaring me. If the invitations were misprinted or something, just tell me."

I cleared my throat, wishing something simple like a reprint could solve her problems. "I didn't want to tell you over the phone, but Caden and Riley were called away for an emergency." I leaned close to whisper. "Nan is dead."

Chloe sucked in a choked breath, drawing the curious stares of those around us. I lifted a hand, hoping to help her remain calm. When she spoke in a low tone, her voice carried a tremor. "I can't believe this. How awful."

Myriad emotions danced in her eyes, from horror to worry to recognition. I nodded, letting her know I understood her feelings. I glanced from her plate to mine, noting that we'd both eaten more than half of our dinner. "If you're finished, let's talk about this in the car."

She glanced over her shoulder at the full café and lifted her hand, signaling our server. Minutes later, we slipped past Brandon while he was immersed in his meal, and we no longer had to worry about being overheard. We escaped the cozy restaurant, emerging into the crisp fall air, and I filled my lungs

Once we were in the truck, I started the engine to warm us and turned to my friend. She blinked rapidly and shook her head. "Poor Nan. I saw her only two days ago for my final fitting, and she was just fine. She's too young for a heart attack, isn't she? Was it a car accident?"

I clenched my hands. "It was neither of those, Chloe. Nan was... murdered."

Her harsh breath echoed in the quiet truck, and she quickly covered her mouth, her eyes wide in horror. "What?" She shook her head rapidly before she whispered. *"No."*

My insides doubled over as I considered the rest of what I needed to tell her. I wanted to allow her to get over the shock of hearing about Nan before I imparted the rest of my news. But there was no time for that.

I raised my gaze toward the roof of the truck, silently asking the Goddess for help. "Someone stabbed her with her own shears," I added softly as I glanced at my friend.

Despair overtook her features, and she blinked back tears. "I can't even... This is utterly unbelievable. Who could do such a thing?" She placed a hand over her chest and struggled to inhale. "I feel horrible even thinking about my dress, but *what do I do?* I don't know if I can wear it now."

I took her hand, pressing it between both of mine. "Chloe." I paused and exhaled my weariness. "You'll need to find another wedding dress."

She stared at me for a long moment before she slowly nodded. "That would be best, wouldn't it?"

I squeezed my eyes shut before looking at her again. "It's your only option because Nan was—oh, Chloe. I don't even know how to tell you." I hesitated and then let the words rush from me. "She was wearing your dress when she was murdered. It's ruined."

Chloe gripped her throat as though my words had strangled her. Tears flooded her eyes, and I felt like the worst friend ever for telling her such news. I slid an arm about her shoulders and awkwardly tugged her closer. "I'm so sorry," I whispered. "I would have given anything not to tell you."

"*My dress?*" A sob escaped her. "How can this be, Evie? *How?*"

I leaned away from her, commiserating with a heart-felt look. "It's so tragic. For her and her loved ones. But for you, too. I don't know what to say. There's nothing that will fix this."

Chloe wrapped her arms around her stomach and leaned forward, breaking my heart all over again. I patted her back. "It's going to be okay. Just try to breathe for now."

She choked out her words. "Maybe this is a sign that the time's not right to get married."

I frowned. "That's absolutely untrue. And you know Nan would agree with me. It's tragic that you won't be able to wear her dress, but imagine how she'd feel if she knew her passing had ruined your wedding. You need to move forward. For her. For you, and for Riley."

Chloe nodded, tears spilling over, her vulnerability laid bare in the harsh light of tragedy. "I guess you're right, but heaven help me, I can't even think right now."

I consoled her with a small smile. "Then I'll take over until you can. I think the best thing is to contact your wedding planner. Taylor has all kinds of connections, and I bet she can help us."

She wiped her tears with the back of her hand. "Yeah. Maybe so. Taylor's amazing."

The tension inside me loosened. "She is. Let me handle things for now. I'll call her first thing in the morning and schedule a meeting. I'm certain once your mom hears what happened, she'll let me leave the bakery to go with you no matter how busy we are."

Chloe sniffed and placed a hand on her forehead. "Would you mind dropping me off at my mom's? My head is killing me, and I need to tell her what happened, too."

"Of course."

I shifted the truck into reverse to back out of the parking stall at the Gooseberry Café. We both fell into our thoughts on the way to her mother's house and arrived a few minutes later. I stopped in the driveway and caught her arm before she climbed out. "Hey, wait a second."

I dug in my purse until I found the small brown bottle carrying the headache potion my next-door neighbor Gertie had taught me to make. "Here. Take this. It'll help with your pain.

Her eyes grew misty as she accepted it. "Thank you, Evie. I don't know what I'd do without you."

I leaned over and gave her a side hug. "I don't know what I'd do without you, either. Hang in there. We'll figure this out."

She stepped out of the truck and made her way to the house, her shoulders slumped in defeat.

I released a long, slow breath, grateful things hadn't totally disintegrated considering the circumstances. But I'd meant what I said. We'd find a way around the tragedy, and my best friend *would* have a beautiful wedding. I'd make sure of that.

FOUR

B right sun rained down on the sage green Crafts-
man house as Chloe and I pulled up late the next
morning. Taylor's home, a block from the lake, always
had a way of looking like it belonged in a storybook,
with its white trim and dark wood columns. Today,
though, there was a different energy in the air, one
tinged with the recent shadows of our small town's
tragedy.

Chloe parked her car, and we stepped out, our footsteps in sync on the stone paver walkway. The flower
boxes under the windows were filled with dead blooms
from the recent frost, echoing the somber mood that
hung over us. We didn't bother knocking since Taylor's
open-door policy for clients was well known in Honeysuckle Springs.

As we entered, the familiar scent of lavender and
vanilla greeted us, but it was undercut by a tension
that seemed to cling to the walls, and I assumed Taylor
would have heard about Nan by now.

In the front hall, we found Taylor in conversation with Patricia Lane, a customer who occasionally came into the Cookie Corner Bakery where I worked. Patricia, with her long, dark hair in loose waves and her bohemian top accentuating her curves, looked every bit the laid-back lake town woman she strived to be. Yet, her almond-shaped eyes held a stormy expression that belied her calm exterior.

"Chloe, Evie," Taylor said, her voice a mix of professionalism and genuine concern. "I'm so sorry to hear about your dressmaker, Chloe. It's just awful what happened."

Chloe's expression immediately crumpled. "It's not just Nan." She inhaled, her voice shaky when she spoke. "She was wearing my dress when she died."

Taylor inhaled sharply. "What? No? How could that happen?"

Patricia snorted. "I'll tell you how. That Nan didn't know how to keep her hands off things that weren't hers. And didn't know how to stay in her own lane. Trying on a bride's dress? Shameful, if you ask me. No wonder she had so many enemies."

The comment hung in the air, heavy with unspoken implications swirling around it. I exchanged a glance with Chloe, her green eyes wide with a mix of shock and curiosity, and I wondered what other things Nan had messed with that weren't hers.

Taylor glanced between us, looking uncomfortable. "Patricia, thank you for stopping by. We'll talk more later about the ski resort's season opening," she said, her tone polite but firm. "Together, we'll come up with some great ideas."

Patricia reared back as though affronted, but she didn't put up a fight. As she left, I couldn't help but notice the way Taylor's gaze lingered on us. I expected, unlike Patricia, Taylor understood how the woman's words would continue to upset Chloe, and I was glad she'd sent her on her way.

Once we were alone, Taylor ushered us into her office and motioned to the chairs in front of her desk. "Let's sit down and figure out how I can help."

As I settled into my seat, I noted that Taylor's polished exterior had cracked. Worry lined her face, and her hands held a slight tremor. Her usual air of unflappable control seemed to have slipped, like a mask that had been nudged askew. Her long blond hair, always so perfectly styled, now had strands escaping their confines, framing her face in a disordered halo.

The room was a reflection of her inner state, cluttered in a way I had never seen before. Papers were scattered across her desk, and the neat stacks of files and trays were in disarray. I couldn't help but wonder what had seeped into her sanctuary, disrupting the harmony she so carefully maintained.

Even if I wasn't a person with highly sensitive witchy tendencies, I'd be able to tell something wasn't right. "Is everything okay, Taylor?"

Her eyes met mine with a panicked look. "Of course. Why do you ask?"

I lowered my gaze to her unruly desk, and she immediately began to gather papers. "Oh, this? Sorry. Patricia had a question about a previous event, and I had trouble locating the material. I had to open several files to find it."

Her expression remained composed, but her eyes betrayed a hint of distress. "To be honest, it's been a challenging morning already."

Chloe and I exchanged a worried glance before turning our attention back to Taylor as she finished haphazardly stacking papers and files, pushing them to the side. If it had been anyone else, I wouldn't have been surprised. But not this lady whose middle name was meticulous.

Taylor exhaled a deep breath and focused on Chloe with a concerned expression. "Enough of that. I'm here to help you."

Emotion flooded my best friend's eyes, and I grabbed her hand, squeezing it before I addressed Taylor. "Since weddings are your thing, do you happen to have any contacts in the wedding dress business? Someone who can help us in a pinch?"

Chloe wiped her eyes and nodded in agreement.

Taylor drew her brows in compassion. "Of course. I know several people. Let me grab my information."

She stood, her movements lacking their usual grace, and turned to the shelf of binders behind her. She selected one and opened it on the credenza below, flipping through the pages. "I have contacts for emergency dress fittings," she said, her voice striving for its typical confidence. "I'm sure one or more also sew dresses. We'll find you something beautiful, Chloe."

As Taylor searched, my gaze drifted to the papers she'd gathered and pushed out of our way. I wasn't trying to be nosey, but the bold red letters stating Overdue Notice stood out amongst the other papers and envelopes, jarring me.

I had no idea if the notice belonged to her or someone else, or even if it was years old, but it did make me wonder if that was the cause of Taylor's upset. Maybe she wasn't as financially solvent as I'd believed.

The woman returned to her desk, setting the binder in front of her before tucking a wayward strand of blond hair out of the way. "I think someone on this list might help."

Chloe nodded, her face a mix of gratitude and concern. "Thank you so much. I just can't believe this is happening."

Taylor tapped on the page in front of her with a manicured nail, her professionalism resurfacing, pushing back whatever personal turmoil she was experiencing. "Instead of having you call around, why don't you let me? I'm sure one of these designers would be willing to work on a tight schedule. I'll contact them right away and let you know as soon as I have someone lined up."

My friend and I both exhaled with relief. Taylor glanced between us. "Now, is there anything else I can help with?"

Chloe quickly shook her head. "No. If you can manage this, you'll have my eternal gratitude."

"Mine, too," I added.

The usually composed woman stood. "Wonderful. I'll let you two ladies get on with your day, then. I'll get right on those calls." She glanced across her desk. "And then tackle this mess. I'm sorry you had to see it."

"We understand, Taylor," Chloe said, her voice soft with empathy. "Life gets messy sometimes."

There was a pause, a moment of shared understanding, before Taylor led the way to her front door. I was about to leave without bringing up Patricia's behavior again, but I couldn't let the opportunity pass. I stepped out and turned back to Taylor. "Do you mind if I ask a question?"

She gave me a cheerful shrug. "Of course not."

"What Patricia said bothered me. Was she suggesting Nan deserved to die?"

Taylor's eyes narrowed slightly, a flash of annoyance crossing her features. "Don't listen to her. She and Nan had a complicated relationship, and she tends to blow things out of proportion."

Chloe arched her brow. "Complicated how?"

Taylor hesitated before answering. "How do I put this? I guess I would say they were friends, once. But things soured after Patricia accused Nan of going after her husband. It caused quite a stir."

The implication left me with a chill, one that was quite in proportion after recent events. "Do you think Patricia could have...?"

Taylor held up a hand, cutting me off. "I wouldn't speculate on that. It may cause Patricia serious problems that are unfounded. Patricia is known for her loud mouth, but I believe she's all bluster."

I nodded, realizing I'd probably gotten all the information from her that she'd give. "Good to know. Thanks again for seeing us on short notice."

Chloe nodded heartily. "Yes, thank you so much. I'll be waiting for your call."

Taylor placed a reassuring hand on Chloe's forearm. "Try not to worry. Things have a way of working out, and fifty years down the road, when you're celebrating your anniversary, you'll be able to look back and laugh."

Unexpected awkwardness jumped in, and we all stared at each other wide-eyed. Taylor coughed at her thoughtless statement. "Well, maybe not laugh. But this disaster will be replaced by happy memories of your day."

Chloe and I both nodded before turning and heading toward her car. As she started the engine, neither of us mentioned Taylor's faux pas, and it seemed the less I talked to Chloe about Nan's untimely death, the better.

But that didn't mean I wouldn't mention my suspicions to Caden. Taylor might easily dismiss Patricia as a suspect, but I wasn't. I glanced at my friend, happy to see she didn't seem as distraught as she had when we'd arrived. "Hey, would you mind dropping me off at the police station? I need to see Caden for a minute before I head into work."

She dipped her head in agreement as we drove away. "Of course not. Tell Riley hello for me if you see him."

The fact that she was thinking of other things lightened my heart. "I sure will."

FIVE

T he plain brown brick police station stood unassumingly against the backdrop of my town. Its glass doors reflected the afternoon sun, casting a golden glow on the waxy green boxwoods lining its base. I stepped out of Chloe's car and glanced back with a reassuring smile. "Thanks for dropping me off. Try not to worry too much, and let me know when Taylor gets back to you."

She blinked back tears and nodded. "Thank you for going with me today, and for all your help."

I curved my lips into a warm smile. "Of course. I'm always here for you. We'll get this figured out."

I was resolved to not only help Chloe with her dress but also Caden with discovering the culprit who took Nan's life. A new wedding dress was one thing, but allowing the poor dressmaker to rest in peace would go a long way with Chloe and the rest of the town, too.

As she drove away, I turned my gaze to the charming pitched roof over the entryway in front of me, its thick wooden beams a testament to the town's woodland charm. I pushed through the doors, and the familiar scent of polished wood and coffee greeted me. The station was always a buzz of activity, but today, it seemed more subdued. I suspected it was weighted by Nan's untimely death hanging heavy in the air.

The reception area was currently unmanned, but with Caden and me now a solid couple, I was comfortable walking straight to his office without asking permission. I found him at his desk, his room a sanctuary amidst life's chaos. The window behind him offered a picturesque view of the lake, its surface shimmering under the bright sun. Hills dotted with pines framed the horizon, painting a serene backdrop.

His desk, a solid, unpretentious piece, bore the marks of his busy job, including files arranged in neat stacks and several coffee mugs, one of which he currently had his hand wrapped around as he stared at an open file.

Whatever he read must have been significant because he seemed unaware of my presence. I knocked softly on his door frame, and he jerked his gaze upward, his gray eyes looking like I'd ripped him from austere contemplation.

I winced in apology as I stepped in and closed the door. "Sorry. Didn't mean to startle you. I'd offer to come back later, but I think you'll want to hear what I have to tell you."

A smile softened his features, and he stood, waving me forward. "No sense waiting to see you until later when I have you here right now."

The way he looked at me never failed to send warmth pulsing through my veins. I accepted his outstretched hand and allowed him to pull me in for a tight hug. I soaked in his presence for several seconds before I pushed away and met his gaze. "How are things going?"

Caden released me with a long sigh and returned to his desk. He leaned back in his chair, the blinds casting alternating stripes of light and shadow across his face. "I guess they're going. For one, the scissors used in the murder were wiped clean. No prints, no DNA," he said, his voice tinged with frustration. "Other than that, we've had a few leads in the case, but nothing substantial. Nan wasn't particularly beloved by the people here, but I haven't come across anyone who hated her enough to kill her."

I nodded, absorbing the gravity of his words, and dropped into my usual chair. "I can't say I knew her well. I've only interacted with her when I went with Chloe for a fitting, but she seemed nice enough then."

Uneasiness rolled through me. "But it does leave me with an icky feeling knowing that she'd worn Chloe's dress. Maybe it's just me, but it seems like an impolite thing to do, don't you think?"

He stared at me for a moment and then shrugged. "Sentimental-wise, I guess I can see your point. But it's the psychological reason she was wearing it that I'm interested in."

I released a half chuckle. "I'm interested in both."

He grinned, but it faded as he fixed his gaze on the file in front of him. "The coroner thinks Nan was killed the evening before she was found."

My playful demeanor immediately cooled, too. "Estimated time of death?"

"Somewhere between nine and midnight."

Didn't the woman work normal hours? "Why do you suppose she was there so late?"

He shrugged. "That's what we're looking to find out. There was no sign of forced entry, so it's likely she knew her killer."

I arched my brow. "Or she forgot to lock her shop after closing time."

He dipped his head in agreement. "There is that, too."

My thoughts whirled as I shifted in my chair. "Maybe she agreed to meet someone there that night."

Caden leaned forward, interested in my comment. "Are you suggesting a clandestine meeting?"

I lifted a shoulder and let it drop. "Possibly a rendezvous between lovers. I say this because I've just come back from visiting Chloe's wedding planner with her, and we ran into Patricia Lane. Taylor was shocked to learn Nan had been wearing Chloe's dress, but Patricia had a peculiar reaction. She called Nan shameful and mentioned she often wanted what wasn't hers. Said the poor dressmaker had a lot of enemies because of it."

Caden's eyes narrowed slightly. "That's interesting. There's something else that links her. Patricia's husband, Raul, was the one who found Nan's body. He saw her through the shop window and called it in."

My heart skipped a beat. "Really? That's quite a coincidence. Before we left, I questioned Taylor about Patricia's comment. She said Patricia accused Nan of having an affair with her husband. I wonder if there's some truth to that." I imagined how the crime might have gone down. "In fact, what if her husband was with Nan and a jealous Patricia showed up and murdered her in a fit of rage?"

Caden leaned forward and thumbed the scar running through his brow as he considered my suggestion. "Could be. There's history there, for sure. Patricia and Nan had a public altercation a while back when she accused her of the same."

My interest grew. "What exactly happened?"

He sighed. "Patricia, driven by jealousy, confronted Nan about spending time with her husband. She accused her of having an affair right in the middle of a bridal dress fitting session. Nan tried to keep her cool and denied everything, but Patricia wouldn't let it go. It got heated, to the point the bride's mother called us. Nan could have filed harassment charges, but she declined."

I could almost picture it. The tension, the raised voices, the shock of the other customers, especially the poor bride. "What do you think? *Were* they having an affair?"

He widened his eyes and shrugged. "I tend to ignore unfounded rumors for the most part. And from what I heard, Patricia had accused her previous husband of the same, so it might just be her insecurities."

I nodded as I absorbed the information. "If that's the case, that must have been awful for Nan."

"It was. Nan was professional to a fault. She tried to de-escalate, but Patricia was relentless. It ended with Patricia storming out after we arrived, but the damage was done. It was the talk of the town for weeks."

I found that all fascinating. "You say professional to a fault, but you're forgetting Nan tried on Chloe's dress."

Caden tilted his head from one side to the other. "You might be making a bigger deal out of that than it is."

I blew out an annoyed puff of air. "Maybe from a man's point of view, but I guarantee most brides would disagree. And it's not like Nan and Chloe are close to the same size. What if she would have torn it while trying it on?"

He widened his eyes into a lost expression and shrugged. "She would have fixed it since she's a seamstress?"

I scoffed. "Never mind. I'm not arguing this with you. But I will say Nan wasn't so perfect. Not that she deserved what happened to her. Just that her actions might have pushed someone to murder her."

Caden leaned back, his eyes narrowed in disbelief. "You think someone might have murdered her because she tried on a dress?"

I shrugged. "Dress. Husband. Whatever. Women can be jealous creatures."

A slow grin curved his lips. "Are you a jealous creature where I'm concerned?"

I wanted to remain annoyed with him for arguing with me, but that smile and the teasing look in his eyes melted me. I stood and moved until I was close enough to place my pointer finger beneath his chin, tilting it upward. "Never underestimate a jealous witch."

A deep laugh rumbled from his chest, and he pulled me onto his lap before possessing my mouth with a kiss. "Don't worry, my wild witch. I'll never be anyone but yours."

I grinned and kissed him back before I extricated myself from his grasp. We were at his work, after all, and we'd already been caught kissing one too many times. "I'd better get going before we find ourselves in trouble."

He chuckled. "Probably a good idea. And don't worry. Patricia was already on the list, albeit at the bottom. After talking to you, we'll move her up."

I made it to the door before I remembered the other person I wanted to tell him about. I chewed my bottom lip as I reconsidered Chloe's ex-boyfriend's return to town. "There's someone else, though he's probably not worth mentioning."

"That tells me you definitely should say something."

I wrinkled my nose. "Do you remember a guy named Brandon Simmons? He lived around here a few years back."

Caden paused for a moment and then nodded. "Yeah, I think so. He dated Chloe for a while, right?"

His ability to recall people and events sometimes astounded me. Especially since my own memories had been compromised. "Yes. Him. There's no reason to suspect he might be involved, but Chloe and I ran into him the other night at dinner. He clearly still has feelings for Chloe. And he's not happy about her getting married. The way he'd looked at her had seemed awfully possessive and jealous. In fact, he said something about coming back to her too late. I have no doubt he'd stop the wedding if he could." I frowned. "But killing the dressmaker seems a little too far-fetched, doesn't it?"

Caden nodded slowly. "Yeah, probably. But I'll keep him on the radar, just in case. I should warn Riley, too."

I quickly waved my hands between us. "No, don't say anything to him. I don't want to stir up trouble. Chloe has enough problems right now."

Caden cocked his head as if he disagreed. "But if you believe he could be a threat to Chloe..."

I smiled to lighten the moment. "I think he's more of a threat to Riley, if anything. Though I have no doubt your officer could handle whatever Brandon throws his way."

His rigid composure softened, but the firm set of his jaw told me he didn't quite agree. "I won't say anything on one condition. You encourage Chloe to mention it to Riley. She can keep it lighthearted if she needs to. But give Riley the heads-up."

"That's still going to upset her."

"Not more than she already is, I'd suspect."

I supposed he had a point. "Okay. I'll talk to her." I placed my hand on his doorknob, feeling a mix of determination and unease. "This whole thing is so unsettling."

Caden agreed with a nod. "It is, and Chloe deserves peace of mind. The sooner we figure things out, the better."

His words echoed in my thoughts as I left his office. The murder of Nan Collingsworth was more than a tragic event. It was a tangled web of secrets and lies, and my poor best friend was right in the middle of it.

SIX

While watching one of my favorite mysteries the previous night, I heard the sleuth utter a phrase I couldn't forget during the first half of my day at the bakery. It stuck with me so much that it rolled off my tongue in a whisper when I stepped outside for my midday break. "When at a loss for clues, return to the scene of the crime."

That's exactly what I needed to do, and luckily, where I was headed wasn't too far away. Not only that but stretching my legs would feel good.

Blustery autumn winds nipped my cheeks as I strode across the street and headed for Nanette's Creations, but the cool air worked wonders to help settle and organize my thoughts. My recent interactions with Brandon and Taylor left me with suspicions, but at the moment, Patricia and her husband Raul stood out as the obvious suspects in my mind.

Patricia had certainly made her motivations clear to the community and to me and Chloe the previous day.

And if Raul had been Nan's lover? Well, that could lead to all kinds of complications for him, too. Maybe Nan had threatened to go public with their affair. Or maybe she'd tried to break it off. Either might have sparked his outrage.

I slowed as I neared Nanette's Creations, and the darkness beyond her shop's window reminded me that her life had been extinguished as well as the lights. I approached with an eagle eye, scouring the grounds outside her building, looking for missed clues. Though Caden's staff was efficient and professional, they were also human, and people could unintentionally overlook things.

Unfortunately, I didn't spot anything out of place amongst the foliage in front of her building. I carefully stepped into the garden and cupped my eyes to block out the surrounding light as I peered in through the glass.

It looked much the same as it had previously, minus Nan's body. A chill rolled over me, and I opened my senses, wondering if Nan might still be hanging about. If so, I had experience speaking with ghosts, and she might talk to me.

"Is that you, Evie?"

The sound of a female voice coming from behind startled me, and I whirled around. I didn't encounter Nan's spirit but found Betty Conrad, owner of the Bubbles and Baubles souvenir shop next door, standing just outside her door. Though a potted slender pine partially blocked her from my view, I recognized her sturdy build and salt and pepper practical bob. The bright purple scarf she wore about her neck gave me hope she was doing okay since she'd worn only black for a while now. She'd recently lost her daughter, and her husband was no longer with her. Both were blows that would take some time to recover from.

I lifted my hand in a friendly wave as I stepped away from Nan's window and out of the garden. I strolled closer, wanting to engage in a more intimate conversation since Betty might give me some insight on the comings and goings around their section of town.

"Hey, Betty. It's good to see you."

The older woman released a long sigh, grim lines tightening around her mouth. "Are you sure? I'm starting to wonder if I have a cloud of doom following me around."

I winced, thinking about the loss of Betty's family and now of the business owner next door. "It's terrible what happened to Nan, but I'm sure it has nothing to do with you."

She gave me a half-hearted shrug. "I'm not so sure. Things were looking up a little in my life, and now this." She gestured with her head toward Nan's shop.

My gaze naturally followed hers, just in time to see a lean, rugged-looking guy a little older than me trace the steps I'd taken only moments before. He adjusted the ball cap on his short brown hair and peeked inside Nan's shop.

Betty nudged me with her elbow and spoke beneath her breath. "He's one to watch. If anyone wanted Nan out of Honeysuckle Springs, it's Alex West."

I stepped back from the slender pine to get a better look. With his broad shoulders and muscular arms, Alex certainly wouldn't have an issue overpowering a woman and thrusting scissors into her chest. "Why do you say that?" I whispered to Betty.

Unfortunately, I must have been loud enough that he heard me or something else alerted him to our presence because he jerked his gaze toward us. His expression remained passive as he stepped from the garden and strode in the opposite direction without giving us another look.

Betty narrowed her eyes and nodded. "The Lord says thou shall not covet your neighbor's space, and Alex wanted Nan's prime retail spot more than anything. I once asked why he didn't try to get me to move, and he said my shop belonged in the center of town for tourists. Just like his outdoor rental store. But not Nan. He tried numerous times to get her to leave."

I considered her information, but it was a reach to think he'd murder Nan for retail space. "Where's his shop at now?"

She thumbed over her shoulder. "Out by the Gooseberry Café."

As she spoke, a slender woman with straight chestnut brown hair hanging over her shoulder approached. She dressed casually like many in town, but her skinny designer jeans and high-heeled boots stood out. She lifted her hand in a wave at Betty as she navigated her way past us and inside Bubbles and Baubles, the door chiming as she stepped inside.

Betty dipped her head at me. "Looks like I'm needed. I'll catch up with you another time."

I twitched my lips in annoyance. I hadn't finished our conversation, but I couldn't exactly stop Betty from conducting business. As she stepped into her shop, I made a split-second decision and followed her inside. I hung back, pretending to study a rack of sparkling crystals dangling from silver chains, as she greeted the young woman.

"Welcome to Bubbles and Baubles," Betty said in a cheerful voice. "Let me know if there's anything I can help you with."

Her customer curved her mauve-toned lips into a smile. "Oh my gosh, Betty. I didn't realize this was *your* store."

I cast a sideways glance at the shop owner as she tilted her head in a confused manner. "Do I know you?"

The young woman grinned. "Of course you do. It's me. Whitney Flynn. Ron and Hattie's daughter. I grew up here in Honeysuckle Springs."

Betty dropped her jaw. "Well, I'll be. Little Miss Whitney. You've really grown up. The last time I saw you, you were…"

Whitney's light chuckle tinkled in the quiet shop. "Chubby, unhappy, with no clue about life. Thankfully, all that's changed."

The shop owner nodded, still seeming shocked about the woman's appearance. "Looks like life has treated you well. Are you back in town to see your folks?"

She lifted a crystal champagne flute and examined it. "Actually, I'm here for my best friend's wedding, but I decided to come early and spend time with my parents. Just arrived today." She turned her gaze to Betty and held up the sparkling glass. "I was hoping you might have a selection of personalized gifts for her wedding. Maybe something like this engraved with their names and wedding date?"

Betty nodded. "We can absolutely personalize this for you. Or we also have other things that can be engraved as well. Who's the bride and groom?"

Whitney arched her brow. "Chloe Fields, of course. I'm sure you remember we were friends."

A small gasp escaped me, and I hurried to lift a citrine necklace, looking at the stone as if it was the most splendid thing I'd ever seen. It *was* very pretty, but maybe not gasp-worthy.

Whitney continued talking. "But dang it, I can't remember the groom's name."

I snorted inwardly. Some best friend, if she didn't even know who Chloe was about to wed.

"That would be Riley Weaver," Betty answered.

Whitney snapped her fingers. "That's right. Sweet Riley. I haven't seen him in forever, either. I should take them both to dinner and catch up."

As Betty led the way to another section of the shop to show Whitney more gift choices, I stayed near the necklaces, studying the women from afar. I found it interesting that Chloe had never mentioned her friend Whitney since they were supposedly so close. But perhaps they'd been friends when they were much younger and had drifted apart as the years passed.

My lunch hour slowly ticked away while I waited for Betty to conclude their business. But as soon as Whitney left the shop, I returned to the counter where Betty stood. I pasted on a smile, trying to think kindly of Whitney, who was probably a perfectly nice person. After all, she'd come to town for an old friend's wedding. "Sorry for hanging around. I hope you don't mind, but I'm extra curious about Alex and I don't need to be back at the bakery quite yet."

Betty's friendly smile warmed me. "That's quite alright. I enjoy chatting with you, though I'm not sure what else I can tell you about him."

I gave her a casual shrug. "You said Alex seemed serious about wanting Nan's retail space. Like how serious? Murder serious?"

She lifted a shoulder and let it drop. "In the past, I wouldn't have been so suspicious of people, but after recent events in my life, I'm leery of everyone."

I couldn't say that I blamed her.

Betty shifted her stance. "He started out by asking Nan to relocate. Then moved on to begging. She would sometimes come into my shop afterward, upset at his attitude, arguing that she had as much right to have her business in the middle of town as anyone else."

I nodded, encouraging her to continue.

She leaned closer. "I even overheard him offering to pay her to leave, and it wasn't an insubstantial amount of money. He must have really thought his business would flourish if he was located here. That, or he'd become obsessed with trying to cajole her, unable to accept her rejection."

In my opinion, the fact that she'd mentioned a lot of money and used the word *obsessed* changed my mind about Alex, enough to put him on my suspect list. I expected Caden would feel the same. I nodded slowly, as though contemplating. "That's all very interesting, Betty. I hope you don't mind if I share your information with our police chief."

A twinkle landed in her eyes, and she chuckled softly. "I figured you would anyway."

I curved my lips into a guilty smile. "It's hard not to when we're so close."

She grinned. "I see that pretty ring you're wearing. When are you and Caden planning to follow in Riley and Chloe's footsteps?"

My cheeks heated at the thought. "We don't know yet. We haven't set a date."

Betty clucked her tongue. "Don't wait too long. He's too good to let him get away."

Now that the conversation had turned to my personal life, I was eager to extricate myself. I lifted my watch and acted surprised. "Looks like my lunch hour is over. I should head back. Thanks again for the information."

She nodded. "Anytime, Evie. You take care of yourself, you hear?"

I hurried out the door, walking quickly back to the bakery as thoughts raced through my mind. Early that day, Patricia or her husband had seemed like the most likely suspects. But seeing and hearing about Alex shifted him right up there with the other two, in my opinion.

And who the heck was this Whitney woman? I couldn't wait to ask Chloe about her.

SEVEN

The Cookie Corner Bakery was calm when I returned, with only one customer, as was usual for that time of day. It would pick up again once people ended their work days. I filled my lungs full of the smell of freshly baked goods, grateful for my job, as I headed into the back to remove my jacket and don a fresh apron. I'd never tire of the bakery's comforting aroma that always felt like a gentle embrace.

Once Valerie finished with our customer, she joined me in the kitchen. Chloe's mom was the heart of this quaint bakery and the best boss I'd ever had. A woman I admired greatly.

She untied her apron and slipped it from around her neck, pushing back the few wisps of blond hair that had fallen forward.

I caught her gaze. "Looks like you're headed out for lunch, too."

The hints of happiness on her face faded. "Chloe didn't go to work today, so I thought I'd take her to

Burgers and Brews for lunch. If I can't ease her worries about finding another dress, at least I can keep her from starving."

I released a soft snort. "Good idea. I've noticed she has a tendency not to eat when she's stressed."

Appreciation flashed in her eyes. "You're getting to know my Chloe quite well, it seems."

Warmth spread across my cheeks. "It seems weird that we've only been friends for a few months. I feel like I've known her for years."

Valerie dipped her head in understanding. "When you really click with someone, it can feel that way. Chloe says the same about you. Lucky girls."

Since my boss had paved the way for my question, I couldn't help but ask. "Speaking of friends, I ran into someone else close to Chloe today. A woman named Whitney."

She frowned as she stared at me with a befuddled look. "That name doesn't ring a bell. Are you sure her name was Whitney?"

I gave her a matter-of-fact nod. "That's what she told Betty. You know, it took Betty a moment to remember her, too. Apparently, Whitney's thinned out and grown up since she was last here." I shifted my gaze to the ceiling as I searched my memories. "She said her parents were Hattie and..."

"Ron," Valerie finished for me as her gaze turned thoughtful. "Whitney Flynn, huh? I guess I didn't realize she and Chloe were that close."

I shrugged. "She said she's here for the wedding and that they were best friends. I can't imagine they weren't at least somewhat close if she made the special trip."

My boss snorted. "You must be right. It must have been a while ago, and you know how little girls can be. Enemies one minute and best friends the next."

I nodded as I recalled my younger years, the rivalries, and the friendships. Though I wished I could remember my teenage best friend Aimee in better detail. We'd had some great times together during the summer I'd previously spent in Honeysuckle Springs.

My thoughts turned to Brandon, and I chuckled. "In fact, it seems old friends are coming out of the woodwork for our dear Chloe. When we were at dinner the other night, guess who we ran into? Her old flame, Brandon."

Valerie's eyebrows shot upward before she narrowed her eyes. "That boy broke my poor girl's heart, and their breakup haunted her for months. I wonder what brought him back to town. Surely, not the wedding."

I lifted my shoulders in a non-committal shrug. "He still carries a torch for her."

My boss swung her dark blue coat from a hanger. "I hope he knows he doesn't have a chance. Not now that Riley's in her life. Those two are most certainly meant for each other."

I smiled at the thought of my two friends' love for one another. "Brandon gave it his best shot, awkwardly telling Chloe that he came back too late. But he must know there's no way she'd stop her wedding for him. Especially not if he shattered her heart when he never came back."

She pointed at me. "That's the perfect way to describe how he left her. I didn't like it, but I didn't blame him. Young love is hard to hang on to. He must realize that, too."

I gave her a reassuring nod. "I'm sure he does. He was probably just hoping he didn't have to live with his regrets. Hey, why don't you let me handle the bakery for the rest of the day? I think that girl needs some time with her momma."

A flush stole over Valerie's cheeks. "She's the dearest thing to me, and I'm so happy we're close. I hope some time together will help. If you're sure you have things handled, I think I'll do that. Maybe we can take a relaxing walk along the lake after lunch. Being in nature is sure to help soothe her soul."

It always did for me. "That sounds like exactly what she needs. The whole situation with Nan and her dress has hit her hard."

Valerie sucked her tongue in a chiding way. "It's horrible. Though I can't imagine what would possess Nan to try on Chloe's dress. It's not as if it would even fit her."

I gasped and nodded in agreement. "That's exactly what I said to Caden, and he acted as if I was blowing things out of proportion."

She shook her head in defiance. "Most definitely not. The only person who should have been wearing that dress was Chloe, if you ask me."

Her comment turned my thoughts to the poor dressmaker. "How well did you know Nan? What was she like?"

Valerie released a long breath that stirred her bangs. "She was… complicated. A smart lady. Could be very generous and was on many occasions. But she had a dark side to her, too."

I was delighted to find a useful, easy-to-access source of information and used it to my advantage. "Tell me what you think about this. When Chloe and I were at her wedding planner's the other day, we ran into Patricia Lane. She had nothing nice to say about Nan, even knowing she'd just been murdered. After Patricia left, Taylor told us that Patricia had accused Nan of having an affair with her husband. I wasn't sure I believed it, but after hearing you talk about Nan, it makes me wonder. Do you think it was true?"

She thought for a moment and then nodded slowly. "I wouldn't put it past Nan. She was a woman who liked getting what she wanted." Then she shook her head. "But on the other hand, I just can't see Raul Lane being unfaithful to Patricia. He dotes on that crazy, jealous wife of his."

I mentally ingested that information, wondering if I should cross Raul off my list.

Valerie slid her purse over her shoulder. "Some people can't be happy no matter what. If Patricia would stop and look at what she has instead of worrying about that nonsense, she could be a happy woman."

Her comment brought a moment of self-reflection, and I wondered if I overly worried about things, too. I would have to ponder that more later when I was alone. I wiggled my fingers at her. "You'd better get going. You have a nervous bride waiting on you."

She chuckled, lightening my heart. "I know it's not funny, but I never would have guessed we'd be dealing with *these* kinds of nerves. I hope that handsome police chief of yours finds the evil person who did this. And soon."

I nodded fervently. "Me, too." And I intended to do everything I could to help him.

As Valerie walked to the front of the bakery, I followed. "Make sure to give Chloe a hug from me."

My boss reached for the door handle, but before she could tug on it, a newly familiar face appeared on the other side of the glass. Valerie opened the door, the bell chiming, heralding the arrival of Whitney Flynn. Chloe's friend stepped into the bakery with a confidence that seemed to fill the room, her sophisticated presence a stark contrast to the cozy, homely atmosphere.

Whitney's chestnut brown hair, sleek and straight, framed her face and accentuated her slender figure as she focused on Valerie with a bright, practiced smile. "Hello, Mrs. Fields. Long time, no see."

Valerie, always the gracious person, offered her a warm greeting. "Well, if it isn't Whitney Flynn who's come back to Honeysuckle Springs. Welcome home."

She cocked her head. "Wow. You're the first person in town who's recognized me."

My boss shrugged, seeming unaffected. "I'd know that cute face anywhere."

I withheld a snort at my boss's smooth manner, allowing Valerie to roll with the flow.

Whitney's smile widened as she moved closer, her demeanor friendly yet with an underlying sense of purpose. "I hope I'm not interrupting. I just wanted to stop by and see how Chloe is doing. I heard about the dress disaster."

My gaze slid to the clock on the wall. Roughly thirty minutes had passed since I'd seen her at Betty's shop and already the news of Chloe's dress had reached her. It had to be a record. Especially since Whitney hadn't been in town long.

"Such terrible timing," she continued. "But I think I can help."

I leaned against the counter, curious yet cautious. "I'm sure Chloe would be grateful."

Whitney shifted her gaze to me. "Oh, hello. I don't think we've met, have we?"

I smiled. "I saw you at Betty's a little while ago. I'm Evie St. Claire."

"It's nice to meet you." She offered me a friendly smile that didn't quite warm her eyes before she shifted her gaze back to Valerie. "Anyway, I've done some marketing work for a national chain of dress shops. They're fantastic, and they handle rush orders. It's not the one-of-a-kind dress Chloe had, but they are beautiful."

Valerie nodded, her expression thoughtful. "That's very kind of you, Whitney, though I'd be worried about alterations if she purchased off a website. Wedding dresses can be quite intricate, and the last thing she needs is to fret about it not fitting."

Whitney waved away her concerns with a flick of her hand. "I've picked up quite a bit about fashion and tailoring in my career. I'm sure I can manage the alterations, or at least oversee them."

I arched a suspicious brow. "You're a dressmaker?"

She blew out a quick breath. "Oh, heavens, no. My specialty is marketing, but I do focus on the fashion business. I've spent enough time in shops to have learned a thing or two. If you want to market an industry, you need to know it."

I was pretty sure alterations were a little more complicated than that. I shifted my gaze to Valerie to check her reaction, and she seemed as uncertain as I was.

Whitney seemed to pick up on our hesitation and shrugged. "It was just a thought. Something that might help ease her mind." Her eyes brightened. "You know, many bridal gowns and prom dresses lace with ribbons in the back to adjust for different sizes, too. Chances are if she picks one, it won't need alterations at all. I could point her to the website, if she'd like."

I observed Whitney carefully, wondering at her intentions behind the offer. Was it that she wanted to show off her prestige and knowledge of the fashion industry, or did she genuinely care?

Valerie patted her on the arm. "Thanks for the information. I'll pass it along to her. Can she reach you at your parents' house?"

Whitney's gaze glowed with satisfaction as she dug into her purse and pulled out a small notebook. She jotted on a piece of paper before she tore it off and handed it to my boss. "Here. Have her call me. I'd love to take her to dinner, and this is the website if she wants to check it out."

My boss smiled and tucked it into her purse. "I'll be sure to give it to her. Thanks for stopping by."

Her confident grin returned. "Of course. It was good to see you, Mrs. Fields." She turned toward me with what seemed like a genuine smile this time. "Nice to meet you, too, Evie. I'm sure I'll see you around."

She bid us farewell, leaving the bakery with the same confident air with which she had entered. As the door closed behind her, the atmosphere in the bakery seemed to shift back to its usual comforting rhythm.

Valerie let out a small sigh, turning to me with a thoughtful expression. "She's certainly enthusiastic. Not the unhappy little girl I remember."

Life could be rough, and I'd likely acted the same right after my parents had died. "She seems quite content now, and I'm glad she's managed to find her way."

My boss smiled until it reached her eyes. "Same. She deserves it. We all do. I'd better head out and support my girl until things take an upswing for her, too. I have a feeling it won't be long." She patted her purse. "Maybe an online dress purchase is the answer to our prayers."

I sure hoped so.

As I set about decorating the fall leaf cookies I'd baked earlier, my mind lingered on Whitney Flynn. Her presence added another layer of intrigue to the events surrounding Chloe's wedding. I just hoped she was who she presented herself to be and not someone who'd make my friend's life harder.

EIGHT

T he sun hung low over Skipper Lake as I made my way home. The large oak in front of my little house welcomed me with its familiar, comforting embrace, and the day's events, tangled with mystery and emotion, momentarily faded as I stepped through the front door. The gentle hum of the house, with its creaking floorboards and the soft ticking of the living room clock, offered a soothing counterpoint to my racing thoughts.

I paused, waiting for the sound of scampering kittens, but none came. Mentally, I reached out to Kookie and sensed her snoozing in the direction of my bedroom. I shrugged out of my coat and hung it, enjoying the peace that hadn't permeated the house since Aunt Birdie's kittens had taken their first steps.

For once, maybe all the cats had settled down for a nap at the same time. At the very least, I'd expected Aunt Birdie waiting for a saucer of kitty wine and asking what we'd have for dinner.

I made my way to the bedroom as the faint scent of lavender and sage, remnants of Aunt Birdie's last spell, lingered in the air, mingling with the more mundane aromas of home. Perhaps she'd found a new sleeping spell to give her a break from her babies' wild antics.

Inside my bedroom, I found Kookie and little Momo, who was the spitting image of her momma, curled into balls next to each other. Adorable, all-black Mochi had covered his face with a paw, while the two girls had tucked their noses into their tails.

Kookie roused as I stepped inside, and I placed a finger to my lips, mentally communicating with her. *Shh...let them sleep.*

She stretched and stood, slowly sauntering her way to the edge of the bed. I hurried to snag her before she jumped to the floor, but she was too quick, and the noise of her soft paws landing was enough to stir the others.

Mochi rolled onto his back, exposing his belly, a testament to how safe he felt in his home, and Momo peered at me with her pretty eyes. I petted her, scratching her chin the way she loved, before I scooped up Kookie and headed out of the bedroom, hoping the other two would fall back into slumber.

As I headed quietly down the hall, I whispered in Kookie's ear. "Where's your momma?"

She blinked her peculiar yellow eyes at me. *Don't know. She disappeared.*

Her answer startled me, and I instinctively focused on the red jasper necklace I always wore that connected me with my Aunt Birdie by way of a similar small stone hanging from her collar. Her strong, calm presence reached out to me, assuring me that she was nearby and in no danger.

Likely, she'd sought out a hiding place to escape her wild ones, and I had a feeling I knew exactly where to look. I left Kookie in the kitchen munching on several cat treats, and made my way to the spare bedroom. After stepping inside, I closed the door, hoping to keep my aunt's hiding place a secret.

Carefully, I opened the cracked closet door and peered inside. A smile crept across my lips when I heard soft breathing coming from Aunt Birdie's sewing basket. I hated to disturb her, but she'd prefer that as opposed to missing dinner before I headed out on an evening walk with Caden.

Slowly, I lifted the lid and reached my fingers inside until I touched her soft fur. She grumbled in her sleep, and I shifted my hand to her belly, softly stroking her.

"Mmm... That's lovely, my dear."

A special tenderness that bound me to my aunt stirred in my soul. "You're very soft and warm, and I know how much you love it."

"More than almost anything," she murmured.

I grinned, playing along. "More than bites of chicken?"

Her purrs echoed against the sides of the small closet. "Yes."

I narrowed my gaze and thought harder. "More than chasing squirrels?"

Her voice was stronger when she spoke, but still sleepy. "Of course."

A soft chuckle spilled from me as I came up with a question she couldn't refuse. "More than Cromwell and kitty wine?"

Her eerie yellow eyes flashed open, and she stared. "Sorry, dear one. You've got me there."

I ruffled the fur behind her ears before I stepped back and allowed her to stand and stretch. When she finished, she glanced at me with curiosity. "Why are you waking me? I was having such a lovely nap."

"It's getting late. I thought you wouldn't want to miss dinner."

She jumped from the sewing basket so fast that she startled me. "Is it really that late? Oh, goodness. It was so quiet and dark in there that I didn't notice."

I led the way into the kitchen and opened the fridge, with her trailing behind. "Don't get too excited," I said as I reached for the half-empty casserole dish. "We're having leftovers."

Her purrs of contentment drifted up to me. "That's fine with me. It's my favorite."

As I prepared our meal, Birdie sat on the counter next to me, studying me with an intense gaze. "I thought maybe you'd woken me to say you'd finally filled Caden in on our little secret."

My gaze shot to her, and I sighed in exasperation. "Stop asking. I know I need to tell him about you. And soon. But it's so hard. I mean, what do I say? Hey sweetheart. Guess what? I've been lying to you for months, and you're never going to believe this, but Aunt Birdie is alive. Not only that, but she's living inside Theo's body."

I paused and soaked in the absurdity of it. "He'll either hate me or die laughing. Or both."

Aunt Birdie reached out a soft paw and placed it on my forearm. "Give the man a little credit, Evie. He's aware you're a witch and that sometimes magical things defy the laws of nature as he knows it. I don't think he'll be all that shocked." Her whiskers twitched. "I doubt he'll pass out like you did when you discovered me."

I shot a sideways, chiding look at her. "Not funny. I could have died from a heart attack that day."

Her laughter rang through the kitchen. "You should have seen your face, my dear. Priceless."

I rolled my eyes and focused on dinner. "If you're trying to comfort me, it's not working."

Her mirth settled, and she rubbed against my arm. "You'll be okay, my girl. Stop making yourself miserable and tell him. He loves you, and I'm certain he'll accept everything about your life, including your old Aunt Birdie. You forget. He and I used to be great friends. I can't wait until he knows I can talk to him again. I've missed him."

Her comment brought me back to reality and how much her life had changed over the past few months. If she could manage something so drastic, I could certainly tell my fiancé my unbelievable secret. Then I'd ask for forgiveness, and he'd hug me. After that, we'd be free to move on to whatever the future held for us.

I released a sigh full of pent-up fears and frustrations. "You're right, Aunt Birdie. Telling him the truth as soon as possible is the best thing. I just need to trust in him and our love. Everything will be okay."

Something soft bumped into my leg, and I glanced down to see Kookie looking up at me with loving eyes. "Hey there, little girl. Are you about ready to eat? You'll be feasting on chicken," I teased.

She nodded wholeheartedly.

I grinned. "Good. Go wake your siblings and let them know dinner is ready."

My adorable familiar turned, her tail high in the air with a little curl at the end, and barreled out of the kitchen faster than I'd realized she could run. My chuckle was followed by Aunt Birdie's groan. "Couldn't you have let Mochi sleep a little longer? For once, I'd like a meal in peace."

When multiple footsteps pounded the floor, I winced. "Sorry. I forget how rambunctious he is at times."

She gave me an incredulous look. "At times? You mean always."

I scratched the side of her neck. "Tell you what. Help me tackle the dishes after dinner, and I'll pour you a big saucer of kitty wine before I take all three kittens outside. You can enjoy a nice evening on the porch while it's still warm enough to do so."

The first of her purrs were drowned out by a kindle of kittens rushing into the kitchen, all mewling their excitement. I mean, I like to eat, too, but the three of them gave a whole new meaning to voracious chowing.

I knew one day they'd settle into adult cats, but for now, I intended to enjoy the little bundles of fur, their craziness and all. As I lifted a forkful of chicken casserole to my mouth, my mind drifted between Nan's murder and what the kittens and I could do outside.

Perhaps there might be a spell Kookie and Mochi could help me with. It would exclude Momo, but she didn't seem to mind being a spectator. What would be great is if I could find something that would help me detect if someone wasn't telling the truth.

I gasped at my idea, drawing Birdie's attention, and reassured her with a smile. But seriously, that would be so helpful with this case and to Caden many times in the future. It was most definitely worth looking into.

I could ask Birdie for her help, but she needed the rest. So, I planned to sneak our grimoire out of the house and play with the kittens on the lawn as I perused it. If I came across anything that appeared to be useful, they could lend their magic and help me practice it.

It sounded like the perfect way to spend the evening to me.

NINE

After dinner, I couldn't say I was surprised that Momo preferred to stick with her mother on the front porch, climbing onto the lavender cushion on my rocking chair, as opposed to following the rest of us out the back door. But just like Valerie loved spending time with her daughter, Birdie did the same.

With Kookie and Mochi in tow and my spell book tucked under my arm, I stepped out into the cool embrace of the evening. The garden, bathed in the soft glow of twilight, was alive with the gentle rustling of leaves and the distant chirping of crickets. The kittens, released into the open, immediately began their playful exploration, darting among the flower beds and chasing phantom shadows.

I watched them with a fond smile, envious of their boundless energy and curiosity. The garden, with its fragrant scents and whispering grasses, offered a moment of peaceful respite, a chance to breathe and gather my thoughts under the vast, early evening sky.

As I meandered toward the gazebo near the back fence, the flickering light of a lantern next door caught my attention. Gertie, my sometimes-grouchy neighbor, and a helpful mentor in the art of magic, was tending to her own patch of greenery. Her small, stooped figure, wrapped in a warm jacket with her floral housecoat peeking from beneath, moved with a deliberate, if somewhat arthritic, grace.

"Gertie," I called out softly, not wanting to startle her.

She turned, her face lighting up in recognition as she peered at me through thick glasses. "Criminy, girl. You're going to give this old witch a heart attack."

I grimaced as I headed for the fence separating our yards, thinking maybe I should have been louder. "I'm glad you're here. I brought out the kittens to play while I search for a spell, but maybe it'll be quicker to ask you."

Gertie's gaze drifted to Mochi. "Looks like my sweet boy is behaving tonight."

I rolled my eyes while she wasn't looking. "He's being so good right now, isn't he?"

She shifted her attention back to me as I recounted the recent developments in Nan's murder case, particularly Patricia's potential motive rooted in jealousy and suspicion. Her wise, wrinkled face, illuminated by the lantern's glow, was a picture of concentration.

"It sounds like Patricia's emotions might have gotten the better of her," Gertie mused, her voice full of the wisdom of her years. "Jealousy can lead to all sorts of trouble, especially if it's based on misunderstandings or misdirection, and that woman thrives on both."

I nodded, the weight of her words sinking in. "You know her better than I do. Could she have been pushed too far and something led her to violence?"

Gertie's eyes, sharp behind her thick glasses, met mine. "It's possible. Emotions can be powerful catalysts."

Her advice resonated, reminding me of mysteries that often lay hidden beneath the surface. "I had a thought over dinner. Something that might help. Do you know of a spell that could let me know if someone is telling the truth?"

Gertie's lips curled into a knowing smile. "Ah, seeking a bit of magical insight, are we? I'll admit you've piqued my interest. Come, let's see what we can conjure."

I called the kittens, and they happily followed me into Gertie's backyard. Upon spying his witch, Mochi raced forward with leaps and bounds. Gertie bent as much as she could, and her familiar launched himself into her arms, the weight of his landing shifting her off balance, causing her to take a step back. I quickly reached for her arm to steady her, and her soft laugh echoed into the cool evening air. "Looks like you've missed me as much as I've missed you."

The love between the two warmed my heart, and I knew the day would soon come when Birdie would have to part with her son and send him to live next door. But if he kept up his wild ways, Birdie might not complain much.

I tilted my head in wonder, Perhaps that was Mochi's plan all along. I knew he loved his momma, but the bond between witch and familiar was undeniable.

Gertie and I settled on the padded lawn chairs next to a glass and metal table, and she opened her hands. As opposed to a time in the past, I happily slid the book to her. Before, when Birdie had been alive in human form, the two witches often shared grimoires and practiced together, and I knew Gertie missed those times as much as Birdie.

My mentor flipped open the book to nearly the halfway mark as though she knew the tome as well as her own and began turning pages. She leaned closer to the book, grumbling. "It's hard to read in the waning light."

I focused on the lantern she'd placed on the table, and sent a surge of energy its way. The glow brightened considerably, and Gertie cast me a quick glance of appreciation. "I see you've been practicing."

I beamed. "I have."

She nodded as she turned another page. "Your Aunt Birdie says you have more than a bit of fire in you. I'd say she's right."

I wasn't sure my aunt had meant that in a positive way. She usually didn't when she chided me for it, but maybe deep down, even though I vexed her at times, she was proud of my magic.

Gertie inhaled sharply and tapped the page. "Let's give this one a try. It's not a permanent enchantment and will wane as time passes, so if you don't like it or it doesn't work, it's not a problem."

Before I could respond, she stood and began to pick various herbs from her garden, pocketing several stones as she did. As she worked, it seemed her movements were part of an ancient dance between witch and nature, and I took note of each item she chose.

"Truth is a tricky thing, girl," Gertie said, her voice low and rhythmic as she returned to the table and arranged the items in a circle. I was surprised to see so many different crystals, ones that I most certainly wouldn't find in my backyard or naturally lying anywhere around town. "It's often hidden beneath layers of emotion and perspective. This spell will help peel back those layers."

I narrowed my gaze. "Do you keep your crystals in the garden?"

She chuckled. "What better way to cleanse them than leaving them out under the moonlight?"

I supposed she had a point. Though I'd be afraid someone might wander into my yard and take them... unless I placed a protective spell around them. Obviously, she was a much more experienced witch than me and had likely already done that.

Once she had everything arranged just so, she lifted her gaze. "I'll read the spell and you do what I say, okay? At the end, we'll chant the last verse together. Get Kookie up here so she can help."

I lifted my curious familiar who watched me with eager eyes. The second I put her on the table, Mochi meowed, wanting to be included, so I snatched him, too. Once the four of us sat in an outer circle around the items, Gertie drew the lantern closer and began. "We offer light's soft glow, to set the stage for secrets to flow." She glanced at me. "Circle the sage thrice in the air, let it lay all lies bare."

I did as she asked, casting its fragrant scent around us.

"Sprinkle thyme in a circle round, where only truth can now be found."

One by one, I followed her directions. As I did, her words drifted on the air, gathering energy. The atmosphere around us shifted, the night air thrumming with a palpable sense of anticipation.

Gertie continued. "Place lapis lazuli at the heart, to urge hidden truths to impart. Now, hold clear quartz high, to catch moonlight's grace, to clear the mind and light the space."

At her nod, we both chanted with firm voices. "Let honesty unwind in this space. Let no deceit find a place."

As the spell reached its crescendo, I felt a gentle tug at the edges of my consciousness, a subtle but unmistakable sign that the magic was taking effect. Kookie, who had been watching intently, let out a small, impressed mew, her yellow eyes wide with wonder.

A ripple of knowing passed between the four of us, and Gertie clapped her hands together. "Good job. Now remember, it will wane with time. In order to re-energize it, repeat the last verse with Kookie lending her magic."

Excitement filtered through me. "That's it?"

She nodded as her gaze drifted to Kookie and then to Mochi, who was sitting quietly by her side. "You're doing well with your training, Evie. But remember, magic is a journey, not a destination. Each spell you and Kookie perform together strengthens your bond."

I smiled, stroking Kookie's soft fur. "I can feel it. We're growing stronger together."

Gertie nodded, her gaze shifting to Mochi. "And Mochi here, he's coming along quite nicely. Spending time with an old witch like me has its advantages."

I noticed a flicker of jealousy in Kookie's eyes, and it was clear she didn't like the idea of being outdone by her brother. "Kookie's doing great, too," I reassured her, sensing her need for affirmation.

Gertie chuckled, a warm, hearty sound. "Of course, she is. But a little friendly competition never hurt anyone. It keeps us sharp, keeps us learning."

I focused on my sweet familiar, catching her attention. *Don't worry, Kookie. We'll practice even more. You'll be the fiercest familiar around.*

She stepped closer to me on the table and settled next to my chest. Her purrs vibrated into me, deepening our connection. I stroked her soft fur and placed a kiss on her head.

As Gertie closed the grimoire, movement at the edge of the garden caught our attention. Aunt Birdie, in her black and white feline form, passed by on the lakeside trail, her fluffy tail held high. She was closely followed by Cromwell, Gertie's black market familiar, and little Momo, scampering playfully at their heels.

My lips curved into a smile at the adorable trio. "They seem to be enjoying themselves."

Gertie leaned forward, observing them with a twinkle in her eye. "Birdie's finally got the family she always longed for. It's heartwarming, really. And Cromwell's smitten with her. He's been heartbroken since losing his first witch, but I sense his heart is much lighter these days."

Aunt Birdie, once a formidable witch, now found joy in her new life, her kittens, and her blossoming relationship with Cromwell, and I couldn't be happier. It was a lovely reminder that even during life's trials and tribulations, there were moments of pure, uncomplicated happiness.

Gertie and I chatted for a while longer, until the stars began to pepper the night sky. The air was filled with the gentle sounds of rustling leaves, the soft purring of cats, and the distant hoot of an owl, leaving me reluctant to go home. Gratitude welled inside me for the old witch's guidance. "I've learned so much from you, Gertie. I hope you know how much I appreciate it."

Gertie gave me a sly grin. "Well, dear, life is the greatest teacher of all. And remember, every challenge you face, every mystery you unravel, it's all part of your journey. You're stronger than you know."

Her words resonated with me, a gentle reminder of the strength and resilience I had discovered within myself. She didn't know it, but she'd also given me a gentle nudge to confess to Caden about Aunt Birdie. It was all part of my journey as she'd said.

I bid Gertie goodnight and gathered Kookie and Mochi to head back home, feeling a renewed sense of determination. To solidify my relationship with Caden. And to help solve Nan's murder.

As I walked back to my house, the moon casting a soft glow on my path, I knew that whatever challenges lay ahead, I was ready to face them. The magical world was vast and full of wonders, and I was only just beginning to explore its depths. Gertie was a great reminder of that.

TEN

The evening air was crisp as Chloe and I made our way into Scarlet's Pizzeria, a local favorite known for its cozy ambiance and irresistible aromas. To garner some alone time with my best friend, I'd concocted a double date with Chloe, Riley, Caden, and me, and planned it so that Chloe and I would arrive together first, with the guys heading straight from work to meet us there. Then I could ride home with Caden, and the other two could leave together.

As she and I stepped inside, we were immediately enveloped in the warm scents of garlic, herbs, and baking dough. The pizzeria, with its old-world charm, felt like stepping into a different era. Red vinyl booths lined the walls, their glossy surfaces reflecting the soft, ambient lighting.

We chose a booth near the window, the vinyl cool and smooth as I slid across it. The familiar sounds of the bustling restaurant, the clatter of dishes, and the murmur of conversations created a lively backdrop, perfect for my planned topic of conversation. Nan's murder.

As we settled in, perusing the menu, my gaze drifted across the room. That's when I spotted Brandon and Whitney, sitting together at a table near the back. They seemed engrossed in conversation, their heads close together.

I nudged Chloe with my foot, nodding subtly in their direction. "Look who's here."

Chloe turned to look, her expression shifting from curiosity to surprise. "Brandon? With Whitney?" She studied them for a moment and then blinked her gaze back to me. "That's wild. I didn't realize they knew each other. But I guess I shouldn't be shocked since our high school class wasn't very big. It's a relief though. Now I don't have to worry that he hasn't given up on me."

The waitress took our drink orders while we waited for the guys, and I watched the couple's interaction. "No hard feelings that your best friend is interested in your previous boyfriend?"

Her brows shot upward. "Whitney's not my best friend." Her expression turned into a smile. "You are."

Her claim warmed me. "I meant in the past. She said the two of you were quite close."

Chloe waved a hand between us. "My mom told me the same thing, but that's nonsense. We hung out in the same group for a while in school, but we weren't best friends. It was more like we shared the same friends. That's it."

I shrugged. "Apparently, Whitney saw things differently, but I guess it doesn't really matter. It was nice of her to come back to Honeysuckle Springs for your wedding. Did your mom mention she has ideas to help with your wedding dress?"

Chloe grimaced. "She did, but I'm not sure how I feel about buying online. It seems impersonal, and I loved that Nan was making one just for me."

I gave her a sad smile and sighed. "I know. It's unbelievable how that all went down. But you can't get married naked."

Her look of dismay dissolved into a chuckle. "Can't I? It's my wedding after all."

I grinned, glad my joke had lifted her spirits. "Well, I guess you can. Riley probably wouldn't mind, but it might make things awkward for your guests."

Her laughter faded, but she didn't seem as despondent. "I guess it can't hurt to look at the website."

After the server delivered our sodas, Chloe leaned in closer, her voice low in the bustling atmosphere of the pizzeria. "I take back what I said earlier. It is a little odd seeing Brandon and Whitney together. I never would have pictured it."

From the corner of my eye, I caught movement and turned in that direction, expecting to see the guys approaching. When I spotted Whitney heading toward us instead, I whispered to her. "Hold up."

Chloe stopped speaking and followed my gaze, her eyebrows shooting up in surprise for the second time that evening.

Whitney looked as chic as the first time I'd seen her, dressed in a pink cashmere sweater, short skirt, along with black tights and boots. Her smile was warm and inviting as she reached our booth. "Evie *and* Chloe. I didn't realize you were here, too." Her voice bubbled with enthusiasm as she slid onto the seat next to Chloe without waiting for an invitation.

Chloe, taken aback by Whitney's sudden intrusion, managed an unruffled smile, her manners as smooth as her mother's. "Hey, Whitney. My mom said you were in town."

Whitney nodded enthusiastically. "I'm glad she told you. You have my number, then?"

At my friend's nod, Whitney continued. "Seriously, you should give that website a look."

Chloe flicked her gaze to me before she glanced at Whitney again. "Actually, we were just talking about that. I'll see what they have to offer." She paused to look in Brandon's direction and changed the topic. "We just noticed you with Brandon. I didn't realize you guys were friends."

Whitney drew her brows in surprise. "Really? You don't remember the night us girls met up with him and his buddies, and we all went to the movies? It might have been a few months before the two of you started dating. Anyway, that was the night Marilyn tripped on

Main Street as we were walking and sprained her ankle so badly that one of Brandon's friends had to carry her back to her car. Remember that?"

Chloe gave her an odd look but nodded. "Crazy times, huh?"

Whitney laughed. "So crazy. And look at us now. We're all grown up. Anyway, my mom is friends with Brandon's, and I heard he's been having a tough time lately. I thought some pizza might cheer him up."

My friend eyed her. "That's kind of you. Hey, if I remember correctly, you moved to Los Angeles, right? How do you like living there?"

She gave her a happy nod. "It's been great. I got my degree in marketing, and I've been putting it to good use. But when I heard you were getting married, I just had to come home. I've stayed away too long as it is."

Chloe's smile turned genuine. "That's so nice. It's great to see you again and hear that you're doing so well."

Whitney winked. "You're not doing so bad yourself. Riley Weaver, huh? Is he still as handsome and built as he was on the high school football team?"

Pink colored Chloe's cheeks, but she grinned. "Every bit. When Evie told me that he was interested in me, too, I was really surprised. But we click so well, and I can't imagine life without him."

Whitney's demeanor brightened. "Which is exactly why you need to find a new dress so you can stop worrying and focus on your handsome groom." She rested her phone on the table. "Here, I'll pull up the website and then send it to you so that you don't have to worry about finding it later. I've worked for their company a few times, helping with advertising, and they have a wonderful staff who take pride in what they offer. It's not some cheap, fly-by-night outfit. They're legit."

After sending Chloe the link, Whitney slid her phone across the table to her. "I mean, just look at this one. It's gorgeous."

Chloe leaned in, her initial hesitation giving way to curiosity as Whitney scrolled through various designs. From what I could see, each dress was more stunning than the last, and her eyes lit up with each new possibility. It would be fabulous if my friend found something she loved, something that would take her mind off the disaster of her original dress.

Chloe pointed at the phone and leaned closer. "Oh, look. There you are. I didn't realize you were friends with the owner."

Whitney smiled and sighed. "We aren't. Not really. I've done work for them, and one day when I was in their office, someone snapped a photo of us. Lena loved it because she said it made her look fabulous. She asked for my permission to post it, saying people would think I was a customer, and I thought why not? Honestly, it gives me a chuckle whenever I see it. But that's marketing. It doesn't matter what's real. Only what people believe when they see or hear things."

I couldn't argue with that. And that didn't mean all marketers were deceptive. Their job was to give us something that would grab our attention, and Whitney was certainly pretty enough to do that.

Our discussion was interrupted by the arrival of Caden and Riley, both in uniform. I, for one, was thrilled to see my handsome fiancé, and Chloe obviously lit up when she spotted Riley. But Whitney, who had been animated and talkative, suddenly tensed up. She greeted them with a polite but reserved smile. "Hello, officers. Nice to see you both."

Caden and Riley greeted us in return, their eyes briefly flicking to Whitney before focusing on Chloe and me. The contrast between their official demeanor and Whitney's suddenly cautious attitude was surprising. I wondered if it was because they didn't know her well.

Whitney quickly stood and excused herself. "I don't want to keep you from your date, and I should get back to mine. Chloe, think about those dresses, okay? I really think they'd be perfect for you. Let me know if you need any help."

Chloe offered her a genuine smile full of gratitude. "Thank you so much, Whitney. I think you might have found the solution to my problem."

"I sure hope so." With a final, somewhat forced smile, Whitney made her way back to her table, leaving us with a palpable sense of unease. Her departure, though polite, felt like a retreat, and I couldn't help but wonder what was going through her mind as she rejoined Brandon.

Caden and Riley settled into the booth, their presence bringing a sense of normalcy back to our evening. Now that they'd arrived, we could order, which was great because I was starving. And then we could get down to business. Between the four of us, I figured we had a lot to discuss.

ELEVEN

Out of the four of us on our double date, Chloe was the only one who didn't lift her menu, but watched me with a contemplative look instead. "Evie, did Whitney seem off to you?"

The guys both turned their attention to Chloe, and I leaned in, sensing her unease. "Like what?"

She glanced back toward where Whitney and Brandon were sitting, now engaged in their own conversation. "She's been talking about our past, about moments we shared. But I don't remember them the way she does. It's like she's created this narrative where we were much closer than we actually were."

The doubt in Chloe's voice was evident, her words laced with confusion as she continued. "Why would she do that? Is she trying to rewrite history?"

I pondered the possibilities. "From what I've gathered from you and others, she's a lot different than she was when she left town. People sometimes try to reinvent themselves. Maybe Whitney's trying to reshape her past to fit who she is now."

Chloe nodded, considering this. "That could be it. But it still feels... off."

I shrugged as Riley lifted her hand and kissed it. "You've been through a lot the past few days, and she seems harmless enough. Evie might be right."

She released a long sigh. "Maybe so. I know one thing. I'm starving. Maybe with a full belly, I'll be more rational."

We all chuckled, but I didn't completely dismiss Chloe's musings. Intuition could be our best friend if we listened to it, and there was something about Whitney that rubbed me the wrong way, too. I didn't want Chloe to worry about her, but I'd keep my eye on her instead. After all, what were friends for?

I lifted my menu again. "I agree. I'm hungry, too."

We ordered and chitchatted before Riley turned his focus to Chloe, wrapping an arm about her shoulders and pulling her close. "Hey there. How are you holding up?" he asked, his concern genuine. "Was that woman able to help you somehow?"

Chloe managed a small smile, the earlier surprise and confusion around Whitney momentarily set aside. "Still a bit overwhelmed, but I'm getting there. Thanks to Evie and some unexpected help from Whitney."

Riley raised his brows. "Whitney? Was that *Whitney Flynn*? I thought her face looked familiar, but the rest of her has changed."

Caden directed his gaze toward Chloe's old friend, and there was a subtle change in his expression, a mix of recognition and contemplation.

"Is something wrong?" I asked, curious about his sudden distraction.

Caden turned back to us, his demeanor shifting to something more serious. "Not with Whitney. But there's something you all should know about Brandon."

We all paused, our attention now fully on Caden. The background noise of the pizzeria seemed to fade into a distant hum as we focused on his next words.

He thumbed the scar running through his brow. "I've been doing some digging into Nan's connections, trying to piece together her interactions before her death. And Brandon's name came up in a way I didn't expect."

Chloe's eyes widened in surprise. "Brandon? How could he be involved with Nan?"

Riley, who had been quietly observing, dipped his head in agreement. "It's a lead we're following up on. I didn't want to say anything and upset you, Chloe, but Caden says you need to know."

I was ready to ask for more information just as the server arrived with our dinner. The revelation hung in the air, heavy with implications, along with the aroma of freshly baked pizza, and I patiently waited until we were alone again.

Once the server left us, Caden leaned forward with an intense expression, capturing our undivided attention. "I've uncovered something about Brandon that might change how we look at this case. In the past, Nan tailored a jacket for him. Apparently, he sold it back to her, and she added it to her rental collection."

Chloe and I exchanged a quick, puzzled glance. The connection seemed tenuous, but Caden's demeanor suggested there was more to it. "That could apply to any number of people," I said.

Caden met my gaze, and our shared energy flared in my heart. "True. But the interesting part is the date Nan wrote the receipt and tagged it for her collection. It was the day of her murder, which makes it a lead we can't ignore."

Chloe's expression shifted from surprise to a troubled frown as she leaned in closer. Her green eyes reflected the flickering candlelight on our table, and when she spoke, her voice was laced with concern. "This is unsettling, to say the least. I know I haven't seen him for a while, but I can't imagine him being involved in something like this."

Riley reached out and placed a reassuring hand on her arm. His usual easy-going demeanor had given way to a more protective stance. "People can change, Chloe. Sometimes for the better. Sometimes for the worse. Or sometimes, they've been hiding a darker side of them all along."

She nodded, but her gaze remained troubled. "I'm worried that Brandon still has feelings for me. He made it pretty clear he did. What if his actions were somehow driven by those feelings?"

Riley's expression hardened, a hint of possessive jealousy creeping into his features. "It's just a lead, Chloe, but we're taking it seriously. Until he's cleared, I want you to stay away from him. If he bothers you, call me that instant, okay?"

Chloe seemed reassured by Riley's support yet visibly shaken by the potential implications. Still, she managed a small, grateful smile. "Thank you, Riley. I will. I promise. I just hope this is all a misunderstanding."

For several moments, it seemed we each fell into our thoughts, processing the implications of Brandon's connection to the crime scene while we ate. If Brandon had murdered Nan, I couldn't imagine it would have anything to do with Chloe. For Brandon to have known Nan was wearing Chloe's dress, he must have followed Chloe to the shop to know she'd employed Nan in the first place.

If that was the case, he might have been following my best friend for weeks. *Even months.*

That thought left me with a chill. Surely, if it was Brandon, there must be another reason why he'd want Nan dead.

Unable to accept that resolution, I broke the brief silence and turned the discussion toward another potential angle in the investigation. "Honestly, I'd be more inclined to believe Patricia or her husband Raul was behind the murder. There was tension between them, especially regarding Patricia's spouse. And from what I can tell about Patricia, her emotions simmer just below the surface, making her easily riled."

Caden nodded, his expression thoughtful as he took a sip of his soda. "Yeah, their history is full of commotion. In fact, while looking into their interactions, we found ambiguous text messages between the two on Nan's phone that might have been veiled threats. And several others brought up Raul, with Patricia telling Nan to back off."

Riley chimed in, his tone analytical. "Like you said, Evie. Patricia's known for her emotional outbursts. She's made scenes at town events before, publicly accusing Nan of inappropriate behavior with her husband more than once."

Chloe listened intently, her earlier apprehension giving way to curiosity. "Do you think Patricia might have misconstrued their relationship? Maybe she thought there was more to it than there actually was."

Riley shrugged. "Maybe. But we can't discount the fact that Raul is the one who discovered the body."

Chloe gasped. "Seriously? Wow. That's... wow. Do you think he worried Patricia did something to her? Or maybe *he's* the culprit?"

Caden's eyes widened at Riley's revelation, and I bit into my bottom lip, wondering if the chief had a problem with his officer mentioning confidential information. He placed a firm hand on the table and glanced at each of us. "As a reminder to everyone, this conversation goes no farther than this booth. Understood?"

Chloe nodded as I responded. "Of course."

Caden seemed appeased as he continued speaking in a low voice. "If the coroner's time of death is correct, Raul Lane has a solid alibi, so it's not likely him. He was one of the first people we interviewed, and he seemed to check out. When I questioned him about his wife's accusations, he denied there was ever anything between him and Nan, other than she's helped him with alterations."

I narrowed my gaze. "So, they did know each other. And just because he has an alibi doesn't mean he doesn't know anything. He could be protecting his wife."

Caden sighed. "Yes, that's entirely possible."

With Patricia being top of my list, she'd be one of the first people I'd test my new spell on. She had the motive, the means, and likely the opportunity. "Did any security cameras capture Patricia in the area?"

Riley shook his head. "Not that we've found. Though there is one person who was seen nearby earlier that evening. Alex West."

I dropped my jaw, remembering what Betty Conrad had told me about him. After a quick glance at Caden, I focused on the other two. "I don't know if you've heard, but Alex West *really* wanted Nan's shop space. Betty actually used the word *obsessed* when saying how much he wanted it and how hard he pursued her to give up the location."

Chloe's expression sharpened with interest. "The guy who runs the outdoor gear rental shop?"

I pressed my lips together and nodded. "That's the one. He even made offers of significant cash."

Riley leaned forward, his brows furrowed in thought. "That's a motive, alright. Financial gain, especially if he was that determined to expand his business into her space."

Chloe turned to him, unconvinced. "But would someone really go to the extent of murder just for a prime retail spot?"

Caden huffed softly. "Outdoor sports tourism brings in a lot of revenue in our little town. And people have committed horrendous crimes for much less. Desperation can drive people to extreme actions, especially if he believed that space was the only answer to his problems."

Riley squeezed Chloe to him. "Don't worry. They're all on our radar now, and we'll interview them soon. Brandon should be coming in tomorrow. You just worry about the wedding and leave the rest to us."

She gave him a grateful smile. "You're truly my hero."

His cheeks blushed bright red, leaving Caden and me with a chuckle.

The light humor was a relief after our serious conversation, but I could see the concern in my best friend's eyes, a reflection of the unsettling reality that the murderer could be someone we all knew, someone who walked the same streets and frequented the same places as us.

As the conversation wound down, I found myself deep in thought. I resolved to follow up with Patricia on my own. The new truth-revealing spell I had learned from Gertie could be the key to discerning whether Patricia's accusations and outbursts were founded in reality or mere jealousy-fueled fabrications.

Alex would be second on my list. Unless I ran into Brandon first.

The thought of using my newfound magical abilities in the investigation brought a mix of excitement and apprehension. The line between the ordinary and the mystical in Honeysuckle Springs was becoming increasingly blurred for me, and I was right at the crossroads.

We continued to chat as we left and stepped out into the cool night air, the warmth of the pizzeria giving way to the crispness of the evening. Under the starlit sky, we said our goodbyes, each couple heading in their respective directions. The night had been exactly what I'd hoped for, with the added bonus of running into Whitney and Brandon, leaving us with many clues to follow, and I was eager to chase them all down.

TWELVE

The morning sun reflected off the landscape as I drove Caden's truck toward Powder Peaks Ski Resort, filled with the anticipation of the day ahead. My mischievous familiar Kookie perched on my shoulder, excitement oozing from her in advance of our adventure.

I'd found myself with plenty of time to pop in at the ski resort since my early morning dentist appointment was over, and Valerie was not expecting me until noon. I hoped to find Patricia in her office since I'd concocted the perfect reason to visit on the way over.

Valerie hadn't sent me to see if we'd be providing cookies for the ski resorts' season opening event this year, but she'd mentioned we likely would. I was certain she wouldn't mind when I told her I'd already checked in with them.

I glanced at Kookie as I traveled along the scenic route leading to the resort. "Let's hope our lie detection spell we learned from Gertie will work. If so, it's our chance to see if Patricia is hiding something about Nan's murder."

Kookie flicked her tail in anticipation. *It will work. I felt it's magic.*

I grinned as I remembered the delicious feel of its power in my veins. "I think so, too."

The towering evergreens and the rustic ski lodge came into view, leaving me in awe of their beauty. The resort nestled in the mountains was serene during its off-season with few cars in the parking lot, though I expected it would be bursting with activity as soon as there was enough snow.

I parked next to a white sedan and shut off the engine. Kookie jumped from my shoulder, and I held her up to face me. "Remember, we need to be subtle. Patricia can't know we're using a spell. Your job is to help bolster our magic and to see if you sense any change in her demeanor as I talk to her. We'll compare notes afterward."

Curiosity flickered in her eyes as she cocked her head. *What does "compare notes" mean?*

I smiled and kissed the top of her head. "It means we'll tell each other about what we thought and noticed while we're in there."

Kookie responded with an understanding purr. *Let's make magic.*

I grinned at her eagerness. "Let's do it." I reached into my pocket and withdrew the slip of paper with the final words of the spell written on it. "I wrote them down just to make sure I don't mess it up."

She nodded in approval as I held out my hand, and she placed her paw on my palm. I took a moment to center myself and began. "Let honesty unwind in this space. Let no deceit find a place."

A swish of energy flowed through me, followed by the sound of Kookie's happy purrs. She turned her gaze to the impressive lodge, and I knew my little kitty was ready to play her part. I hoped she knew how much her instincts and magical connection meant to me.

I held Kookie tightly against me and stepped out into the brisk autumn air, heading toward the lodge, ready to face whatever lay ahead. Today, we were not just a witch and her familiar. We were detectives on the trail of hidden truths, armed with magic. That thought left me with a grin and filled me with determination.

The entrance of Powder Peaks Ski Lodge loomed before us, its majestic cedar and stone façade exuding a sense of dormant grandeur. Kookie and I stepped inside to an eerily quiet lobby that echoed our solitary footsteps, and I glanced around, looking for someone who could point me toward Patricia's office. But we were all alone.

The front door *had* been unlocked, which I assumed meant they were open for business, and I hoped no one would mind that we'd come inside.

The towering stone fireplace, which would be crackling with warmth during peak season, now stood cold and silent. The plush leather chairs and couches were neatly arranged but unoccupied, adding to the sense of stillness.

I looked down at Kookie, sensing her apprehension. "It's a little spooky, huh?" I whispered.

She agreed with a nod and then turned her gaze outward, sniffing as though that might help her sense danger. I highly doubted we'd encounter any, but we were on our way to question a potential murder suspect, so one could never be too careful.

We made our way through the lobby, where I spotted a small sign pointing us down a hallway to the ski lodge office. I headed in that direction, passing colorful ski posters and vintage gear on the walls, causing me to wonder how long the ski resort had been operating. And more so, how long had Patricia worked for them?

When we reached the office at the back of the lodge, I found the door partially opened and peeked inside. A teenage girl with long, curly red hair decked in a long-sleeved anime t-shirt sat at a desk, talking on the phone. From the tone of her voice, it didn't sound like a business call, so I stepped forward.

She glanced up as she spoke into the phone. "Hang on, Tricia." A bright smile curved her lips when she spotted Kookie. "Can I help you?"

I wasn't sure why, but I spoke quietly. "I'm here to see Patricia."

She glanced between me and Kookie and then thumbed behind her. "Sure thing. Just head on back. She's in the office on the right. Cute kitty. I love cats."

Kookie's purrs rang out, and I grinned. "Me, too. They're the best."

I didn't want to linger and risk having her question my intentions, so I stepped past the side of her desk and strode to the three doors down the hall. Only one was on the right, so I knocked softly and entered when Patricia called out to invite us in.

Patricia sat behind her desk, clad in a russet flowing blouse that accentuated her loose brown hair hanging over her shoulders. Her brows rose in surprise. "Well, hello, Evie from the Cookie Corner Bakery. What brings you here?"

We'd had short conversations a few times when she'd stopped in for cookies, but I was surprised she remembered my name. "Hi, Patricia. I'm actually here on bakery business. Valerie mentioned that we usually provide cookies for the ski resort's grand opening event, so I stopped by to discuss the details and get an idea of what you'll be needing this year."

Patricia's expression brightened. "Ah, yes, Valerie's delightful treats. They're always a hit at our events. Please, have a seat."

The office was a cozy reflection of the lodge's rustic charm, with wooden walls and comfortable furniture. Photos of the majestic ski slopes, covered in pristine snow, adorned the walls, leaving me pondering if I should give the sport a try in the upcoming season. Which also made me wonder if Caden had ever been. It might be a fun date.

I sat down, and Kookie settled quietly on my lap, her eyes observant and alert. I could feel her focus, ready to assist in our subtle investigation. The thought occurred to me that perhaps I should make up a little lie to explain her presence, but Patricia didn't seem to care, so I didn't bother.

Patricia lifted a file from the small stack on her desk, and her demeanor shifted to one of a savvy business-woman. "The grand opening is quite a big deal for us. I've been working on numbers and plans all this week. Calling Valerie was on my list of things to do, but I'm happy that now it's been taken care of for me."

She seemed quite delighted by that fact, and I nod-ded happily, wondering how to steer the conversation toward Nan. "From what I hear, it's a highly anticipated occasion."

Patricia closed the file in front of her and opened an-other, mumbling as she did. "It is, indeed. Let's see. Last year, we ordered five hundred cookies. We're expecting approximately the same number of people this year, so I think our order will be the same."

I gave her a bright smile. "I'm sure Valerie will be pleased to hear that."

She tapped her bright nails on the desk and nar-rowed her eyes in contemplation. "I've been thinking though. This is our fiftieth anniversary, and I'd like to do something special. I've heard others talk about the cute decorated cookies the bakery has now. Perhaps I should ask Valerie to do something special just for us."

Warmth crept up my cheeks at the thought of people complimenting my creative works. "Are you talking about the detailed fish cookies and the Skipper Lake Monster cookies?"

She grinned and pointed a finger at me. "Yes, those. Do you think Valerie would agree? I'm sure they'll cost more, but we should splurge a little this year, don't you think?"

I tried to keep from gushing with happiness. "Actually, I'm the one who creates those, and I'm sure Valerie would love to accommodate you. If you'd like, we can come up with a design just for you."

Patricia clapped her hands together. "That sounds absolutely wonderful."

I couldn't agree more. "Do you have any suggestions as to what you'd like? Or should I come up with ideas?"

Her lips curved into a smile. "I'd be happy to leave it all up to your creative genius. I'm sure you'll find something perfect."

Kookie's claws pierced my jeans and stole my attention. I glanced downward, and her disappointed expression caught me off guard.

I thought we were going to question her.

She was right. I'd been waylaid by Patricia's pleasant demeanor, and the subject of cookies was one I could never resist. I stroked Kookie's fur and gave her a small nod. *Thank you for the reminder.*

Her annoyance softened but didn't completely disappear, and I refocused on Patricia, who nodded at

Kookie. "Beautiful kitten. They're always so cute when they're little."

I bristled at her comment, wanting to tell her that adult cats were also adorable, but I let it pass and gave her a small smile instead. "You know, when I saw you at Taylor's office, I didn't realize you oversaw the ski resort's public relations. That must be why you were visiting her."

Patricia waved a nonchalant hand. "Oh, yes. Taylor's fabulous. She's great at coming up with unique party ideas and helping me pull everything together. How's your friend Chloe?"

My satisfaction flowed freely. She'd taken my bait and given me the perfect opportunity to question her. I feigned a worried expression, which wasn't hard since my friend was constantly in my thoughts these days. "Chloe's managing to hang in there. I know you didn't care for Nan, but it's such a tragedy to have Chloe's dress ruined so close to her wedding."

Pity filtered into her gaze. "Yes, that is regretful. Though other than business needs, I doubt anyone will miss that woman."

I exaggerated a wince. "Ouch. I didn't really know her. Was she that bad?"

"Worse," she said in a leaden voice. "It's like I said that day. She was always after things that didn't belong to her."

I decided to take a chance and delve deeper. "I re-member there was some talk about a public disagreement between you two. It must have been a misunderstanding, right? What was that about?"

Patricia's expression tightened. "Nan had a way of getting under people's skin. Our disagreement was unfortunate, but it was nothing more than a professional clash."

Kookie stiffened in my lap as my stomach clenched, almost to the point of stealing my breath. I swallowed, not realizing the spell's effect when in the presence of lies, would be so strong.

And it wasn't as if I needed the spell to point out Patricia's falsehood. Everyone said the clash had been over her husband, not some business quarrel.

I nodded, giving the impression of understanding. "I'd heard you and your husband had been clients of hers in the past. Though I expect that applies to many in town. Did he end up having trouble with her, too?"

Patricia's composure faltered momentarily, and her gaze flicked to a photo on her desk of her and a dark-haired man with a full mustache. "My husband did commission a few pieces from her, but most of that business was handled through me."

Kookie squeaked as my stomach tumbled. More lies. "Right. He'd only need to be there for fittings and such."

"Exactly."

I stroked my kitty's fur, hoping to ease her distress as I dug deep for an empathetic tone. "You know, the day Nan died was so awful. I'll never forget being at the park when I heard about her death. I imagine you were at home with your husband. How did he take the news?"

Her gaze grew wary. "Actually, I was here at the resort preparing for the upcoming season. I'll admit it was indeed a shock. But to answer your question, I have no idea how he took the news or if it affected him at all."

I leaned forward slightly, maintaining gentle eye contact. "This must have been emotionally taxing for you, especially with the history you shared. Please don't take this wrong, but aren't you worried some might suspect you?"

For a split second, Patricia's carefully maintained composure slipped, revealing a flicker of vulnerability. "It's been difficult," she admitted, her voice softer. "Nan and I had our differences, but I never wished her that kind of harm. As for suspicions, I suppose it's natural for people to talk, but I have nothing to hide."

I'd gone as far as I dared push her without Caden around, so I shifted directions. "I suppose everyone is trying to piece together what happened. Have you heard any theories or rumors?"

Patricia's demeanor chilled, and she focused on me with a piercing gaze. "People talk, as they always do in small towns. I've heard rumors and theories, but nothing concrete. It's all speculation at this point."

She glanced at her watch. "Besides, she's not a subject I particularly care to discuss anyway. I don't mean to seem rude, but I need to get back to work. Please tell Valerie to call if she has any questions."

I quickly gathered Kookie into my arms and stood. "I'll do that. If you don't mind, I'll mock up some designs for the cookies and send you the pictures. That way, you know what you're getting."

She gave me a curt nod. "Sounds wonderful. Thanks for stopping by, Evie. You and your kitty have a good day."

And just like that, we were more or less kicked out of her office. But that was okay. Even if I hadn't learned everything I'd wanted, I knew more than when I'd arrived. Specifically, that woman wouldn't hesitate to lie if she thought it would save her. And second, that spell was a doozy.

As Kookie and I made our way down the hall toward the lobby, the quiet of the ski lodge enveloped us once again. "Are you okay?" I whispered.

My tummy hurts.

I blew out a steadying breath. "Yeah, mine, too. Sorry about that. I wish Gertie would have warned us."

She rested her head on my arm. *I'll be okay.*

I smiled at my adorable little investigator. "Patricia was lying practically the whole time, wasn't she?"

Kookie's gaze turned fierce. *Ever since you mentioned Nan's name.*

"I knew it," I whispered. "She has guilt written all over her. I can't wait to tell Caden. He needs to press her harder for answers. I bet if he does, she'll cave and confess."

My pretty kitty gave me a resolute nod, her bright yellow eyes flashing. *Can I come with you to see Caden? Or is it a "date"?*

She hated it when I excluded her, but this time, I wouldn't disappoint her. I snuggled her close. "Tonight, it's a date for three. You, me, and Caden."

Kookie's eyes flashed with happiness. *Yes. Are you going to tell him about my momma then?*

Her question flipped my stomach worse than it already was. "Not tonight. We have other more important things to talk about. I'll worry about that another time."

She seemed unconvinced, but eventually, her purrs won out. *A date for three...*

THIRTEEN

The evening sun dipped low over the horizon, reflecting off the serene lake behind my house as Caden and I strolled along the trail that circled much of it. The crunch of fallen leaves under our feet marked our passage through the beautiful scenery and the earthy scents of autumn wafted on the breeze, refreshing my soul.

Kookie was nestled in Caden's arms and seemed to be enjoying the outing as much as we were. Every so often, she would climb up and give him a little kitty kiss on his chin, causing him to chuckle softly. The times like this when his gentle and affectionate side emerged were my favorite. Though seeing him in full uniform left me with a thrill, too.

Sometimes, I found it hard to believe he'd waited for me for so many years, never knowing if he'd ever see me again. It broke my heart a little to think about it. I'd been cursed, or blessed depending on how I looked at it, having no memory of him to pine over during our time apart.

But we were together now, and that's all that mattered.

Caden's hand found mine, our fingers intertwining in a comfortable, familiar gesture. We walked in companionable silence for a few moments, each lost in our thoughts.

I hated to disturb the moment, but the urge to tell him about Patricia's lying eventually became too much to contain. "Kookie and I learned something interesting today."

At the sound of her name, Kookie's eyes brightened, and she mewed in agreement. Caden chuckled at her response and touched the tip of her nose. "I'd ask this little cutie what happened, but I'm afraid I wouldn't understand her."

I smiled at my sweet baby. "I'm sure she'd love to tell you, too. But I'll explain for us both."

It only took a moment to fill him in on the spell she and I had done and how we'd planned to use it on our suspect. "I'd talked to Patricia for quite a while with no sensation at all, but the minute I changed the subject to Nan, Kookie and I were both hit with a nauseating sensation, telling us she was lying."

He glanced at me with concern. "That sounds like a rough spell. Are you sure you should be doing that?"

I waved away his comment, though I still felt guilty that Kookie had suffered, too. "We're fine now."

My familiar interrupted me with her thoughts. *Tell him about her husband. That really made my tummy hurt.*

I nodded at Kookie and continued talking. "The worst of it hit us when I asked about her husband's connection to Nan. She said it was only professional, but that was all a lie, too."

Caden turned his gaze to the lake with a thoughtful expression, slowly nodding his head. "That's very interesting. I have a question, though. Does your spell prove that Raul was cheating on her with Nan, or only that Patricia believes he was?"

His question stumped me, and I dropped my shoulders in defeat. "I'm not sure. My guess is that the spell tells us if the person we're asking believes what they're saying or not. And Patricia believes he's cheating. Which I guess is nothing new."

I glanced at my familiar, and she lowered her ears, sharing my frustration. "We may need to rethink how we pose our questions, Kookie."

She gave me a fierce nod, and I couldn't help but feel blessed that the Goddess had gifted me with such a loyal companion. "We'll work on that."

Caden's chuckle echoed around us. "I hated to burst your bubble, but I know you want to get the best information possible."

That I did. "Even so, you should keep your eye on her. She talks about Nan being a shifty person, but I think she's just as bad."

As the last rays of the sun painted the sky in shades of pink and orange, we found ourselves at the end of the trail, near my sacred spot. Caden lifted his brows. "Up for a fire tonight?"

I had to admit his suggestion tempted me. "It's certainly chilly enough, but I think I'd rather keep walking. It helps me to think."

He circled us around, heading back in the direction of our houses. "Same for me. Science has proven that when you use both sides of your body in rhythmic movements, like when you walk, it connects both hemispheres in your brain. It's great for problem-solving."

I chuckled. "Look at you being so brilliant."

He nudged me with his elbow. "Me? You're the one who knew it instinctively."

Kookie lifted her head from where she rested it on his arm. *Tell him you're still learning.*

I snorted at her, and Caden glanced between us. "What? Did she say something?"

I met his gaze and rolled my eyes. "She wants you to know I'm still a novice, still learning."

An entertained grin curved his lips, and he stroked her colorful fur. "I understand, Kookie. I guess it's up to me and you to teach her what she needs to know."

She turned her head to look at him and nodded.

I focused on the pines whispering in the evening breeze to resist laughing out loud. "Trust me. I'm working hard."

He met my gaze over her head and winked. "Glad to hear that."

We both fell into our thoughts as we continued to walk, and soon, Kookie laid her head on his arm again, her eyes growing sleepy. The precious soul owned a special piece of my heart, and it warmed me to know that we'd always be connected.

Caden broke the silence, his voice thoughtful. "Evie, I've been meaning to ask you, what's up with Whitney? She seemed awfully nervous when we ran into her at Scarlet's."

I pondered his observation, recalling Whitney's demeanor. "Well, police chiefs can be quite intimidating, so it could be that. But honestly, I'm not sure what to make of her either. She claims to be Chloe's best friend, talking about shared memories that Chloe says never happened. Like I told Chloe, my best guess is that she's pretending to be the person she wished she was back then. Reinventing her past along with herself."

Caden nodded, his expression turning more serious. "I guess that could be it. She was just... weird."

I wrinkled my nose and nodded. "I get that vibe from her, too, so it's not just you." I slowed and turned to him. "I'm starting to wonder if Chloe is just unlucky enough to have some unhinged people as previous friends."

He laughed at my response. "I guess that's a warning to you to never stop being her friend."

I smiled at his comment, but my nerves quickly kicked in. "We can joke, but I'm still worried the murder might have something to do with Chloe. The thought of it makes me sick. She's such a kind soul. She doesn't deserve to be caught up in something so tragic."

Caden squeezed my hand reassuringly. "Yeah, I don't like it, either. Riley's more worried than he's letting on, too, but I think Chloe's smart enough to listen and take precautions."

I agreed since it wasn't my friend's first time being involved with a nefarious person. "She's taking your advice and being as careful as she can."

"That's good. There hasn't been a real threat made against her, and for all we know, it may have nothing to do with her anyway."

Kookie groaned in her sleep and shifted, nuzzling against the warmth of Caden's chest, her small gesture a reminder of the simple joys and comforts that life offered, even amidst its complexities.

Caden nudged me with his arm. "You're not the only one with news. I found some interesting information on Alex West."

My curiosity jumped to full alert. "Something that might incriminate him?"

He hummed, sounding uncertain. "Maybe. After some digging, we discovered his financial situation is more precarious than most people realize. His outdoor gear rental business is doing well, but it's not enough to keep up with his growing debts."

I narrowed my gaze in suspicion. "That could explain why he was so eager to get his hands on Nan's property.

The location would be prime real estate if he planned on expanding."

Caden nodded, his gaze fixed on the path ahead. "Exactly. And with financial pressure mounting, people can sometimes make drastic decisions. We already have camera footage of him in the area that night, so we're looking more closely into his activities around the time of Nan's murder. I have you to thank for tipping us off about him."

My cheeks warmed as a grin overtook my mouth. "Always happy to help."

The idea of visiting Alex's store myself crossed my mind, sending my thoughts swirling. "I'm tempted to go visit Alex. I'll take Kookie and maybe we can use our spell to see if he's hiding anything."

Caden's hand tightened around mine. "You need to be careful. Using magic like that isn't without risks, especially if you're dealing with someone potentially dangerous. And I don't like that it makes you sick."

The caution in his words tempered my determination. "I know, but it might be our best chance to find out more. I'll be discreet, and I won't take any unnecessary risks. Besides, you know I have my own ways of staying safe."

I gave him a reassuring smile, hoping to alleviate his worries. "In fact, I believe my magic saved you on at least one occasion."

He sighed, the protective side of him evident. "Okay, but promise me you'll be careful. Only simple, unassuming questions. This case is becoming more complex, and I don't want you getting hurt."

I released his hand and wrapped mine around his bicep, snuggling close against him. "I promise. And you know if I don't behave, Kookie will tell on me."

We reached my house before I was ready to go in, and I sighed. "Time goes so fast when I'm with you."

A sly grin crossed his lips. "Agreed. Why don't you take this little one and put her to bed? And then you and I can spend some time at my house. I'll even make you some hot chocolate to warm you up."

I snorted as I slipped Kookie from his arms. "I'm pretty sure if we go back to your place, I won't find myself getting chilly. Not with you around."

His chuckle was warm and deep, and he gave me a gentle push toward the back door. "Why don't you hurry, and then we'll find out."

I teased him with a soft laugh as I walked away. "We could even make a bet on it. If for any reason I find myself cold tonight, you owe me a hundred bucks."

"Deal," he called after me. "I'll make that bet anytime you want."

I grinned as I opened the door and stepped inside. Pretty soon, we'd be living together full-time, and I couldn't wait.

There was only one big obstacle standing between us and everlasting bliss. Aunt Birdie's true identity, and I needed to tell him. Maybe I would confess this evening. But only after I was toasty warm.

FOURTEEN

D ark, ominous clouds gathered over the mountains beyond Skipper Lake as I left my house after a quick dinner the following night. I snuggled Kookie beneath my jacket and dashed from the house to Caden's truck, a wicked autumn wind blowing the strands of my hair into my face. Inside the cab, I released Kookie onto the seat with a grateful sigh.

The second I clicked my seatbelt in place, my sweet kitten released a familiar meow, asking for me to put her on my shoulder. I snorted a chuckle. "Hang on, little lady. Let me get settled first."

After starting the engine, I lifted her soft body, which wasn't as little as it once was, and placed her on my shoulder. She rubbed her cheek against mine, and I shot a side-eye glance in her direction. "Good thing I love you so much, Miss Impatience."

What's impatience?

A grin curved my lips. "It's when you expect me to do things faster than I can."

Like telling Caden about my momma? She lowered her lids in a thoughtful blink. *Don't worry. You're still learning. You'll get faster.*

Kookie had tossed back the words I'd said to her only a day before when she'd failed to beat Mochi in a race, and the surprise of it caused me to inhale a quick breath. And then choke on it as I tried to laugh.

Her soft paw hit the back of my neck, doing absolutely nothing to help me clear my airway. Since retorting wasn't currently possible, I continued to cough as I nodded my head.

After a few swallows, I could finally breathe again, and I shifted Caden's truck into reverse. "Let's be extra careful today, okay? I don't know if Alex is aware I'm a witch, but I don't want him to know, either. Him not knowing gives us an advantage."

What's that?

I smiled again at her curiosity. "Let's just say it helps us."

My answer must have satisfied her because she didn't argue or ask more questions as I drove through the blustery weather in the direction of the Gooseberry Café. From there, I spotted the green and white sign for Rugged Adventures, Alex's outdoor adventure guide shop, and I turned into the parking lot.

The store was huddled on the edge of town, the brown brick structure looking lonely with not much around it. Though its isolation did allow for a large parking lot. I wondered why Alex couldn't just expand the building, but then remembered he wanted to be in the heart of our small town.

I cranked my neck to face my kitten. "I think this time I should revitalize the spell on my own." Her disappointment filtered through me, and I tugged her from my shoulder. "I think your power might be too strong, little one. Maybe with less, we won't feel so icky if someone lies."

She gave me a hopeful look and nodded in agreement.

I quickly tucked her into my large purse before I repeated the last words of the spell to refresh it. Magic rolled through me, and Kookie squirmed in the bag. *I felt that.*

I peeked in my tote to look at her and rearranged the soft blanket at the bottom. "Of course you did. You're my familiar. You're supposed to sense my magic."

Her purrs vibrated the silent air as I exited the truck, shifting the bag onto my shoulder. I hurried for the door as numerous leaves skittered past, dancing with each other in the wild wind. "I'm glad you're inside out of the cold, Kookie. Today is certainly a chilly one."

She didn't respond, but I sensed her gratitude reaching out to warm me, leaving me with a secret smile. I pushed open the door, and a small bell chimed above me, announcing my arrival. I spotted only one person inside, a middle-aged man looking at a selection of fishing reels near the front of the shop, with Alex nowhere to be seen.

The interior was a blend of ruggedness and professionalism and fit his type of store perfectly. The wood-
en beams overhead had been adorned with sets of skis,
and the stone pillars throughout the shop gave it a cozy,
cabin-like feel. In addition, the smell of coffee created
an atmosphere that was both inviting and adventurous.

I *was* there looking for adventure, but probably not
the kind Alex expected.

Movement nearby brought my gaze to my bag, only
to see Kookie's face peeking above the rim, her cute
little nose fiercely sniffing the air.

I want to see.

I rolled my eyes and did a quick turn, showing her
the lay of the land, before I gently tucked her down
inside my tote, her presence a comforting reminder of
the task at hand.

As I stepped further inside, I took a moment to absorb
the ambiance. Display photos of breathtaking wilder-
ness excursions covered the walls, advertising Alex's
tour services. Kayaks, tents, backpacks, and climbing
equipment were neatly arranged throughout the space,
each item promising a wonderful adventure.

The shop was quiet, the off-season lull evident in
the absence of customers. This solitude provided the
perfect opportunity for the conversation I planned to
have with Alex.

I was here under the guise of purchasing hiking boots
and a jacket for the coming winter. It wasn't completely
a lie. I did need a warmer coat and footwear before the

snow hit, and my excuse should serve me well without drawing suspicion.

I casually made my way toward the display of hiking boots along the wall, keeping an eye out for Alex. A cute ladies' boot caught my attention and I picked it up, testing the weight in my hands. The tread on the thick rubber heels seemed as if it would do well in most kinds of weather, and the Sherpa lining promised to keep my feet warm.

Do I need boots?

I wasn't sure how many questions Kookie had asked that day, but I enjoyed her fresh perspective on life. *No, I thought back to her. Kitties don't wear boots.*

Why not?

I chuckled softly. *Ask your momma.*

The sound of footsteps alerted me to someone nearby. I looked up to see Alex emerging from the back of the store, his brown hair mostly hidden by a khaki ball cap, his athletic build and confident stride unmistakable. I placed the boot back on the display, relieved my trip hadn't been for nothing, and waited for him to greet me.

A few seconds later, his piercing eyes met mine, and for a moment, the shop faded into the background, leaving just the two of us in a silent standoff of sorts.

"Good evening." His voice held a deeper timbre than I'd expected. "Welcome to Rugged Adventures. How can I help you today?"

I offered a friendly smile. "Hi. I'm looking for some outdoor boots for the winter season."

Alex stepped forward, his movements exuding the confidence of someone well-versed in outdoor adventures. He gestured toward the display I'd been looking at. "We've got a great selection for winter hiking. Any particular style you're interested in?"

I followed his lead, acting interested in the boots, but I was more intrigued by what he might tell me. "I'm not entirely sure. I live out by the lake and would like to keep walking the trail during the winter, so something durable and suitable for the local terrain."

He chose a different boot than the one I originally had and held it up. "Something like this should suit you well. What size do you wear?"

I actually liked the tan suede one he suggested and was eager to try it on. "I usually wear eight and a half."

Alex seemed friendly enough as he selected a box from beneath the display. "Have a seat there, and try this on. We want to make sure you have the proper fit."

I reluctantly placed my oversized purse that held nothing but a kitty and my wallet on the floor next to the bench and sat. He laced up one boot before handing it to me and then hovered overhead while I wrangled my foot inside.

I caught sight of my precocious kitten's yellow eyes peeking from the bag as I struggled and froze. With my head down, I shot her a warning look, and she crept farther into the depths of the bag.

Once I had the boot on and tied, I stood, taking a few steps. "You're right. This feels really good. I could walk a long way in these."

He grinned. "Perfect. Let's ring them up. Or is there anything else I can help you with?"

You're doing it again, Kookie cautioned. *Ask him your questions.*

She was right. I'd got caught up in the luxury of comfortable boots, thinking about the many walks I'd be taking with Caden this winter. "Actually, I'd like to see what you have for winter coats. I'm afraid the one I brought from the city won't be warm enough."

"No problem. Let me show you what we have."

I hurried to shove my foot into my shoe and stand before following him toward several racks of winter coats. He glanced between me and them and chose a cute tan jacket with a white sherpa lining. "This will be good for being out and about. Do you ski at all?"

I quickly shook my head. "Never tried it. But I was near the ski resort the other day and thought it might be fun."

Alex grinned. "I bet you'd like it." He swiveled and lifted a turquoise and dark blue ski jacket along with a lime green one. "What about one of these? You could wear them hiking or skiing."

I set my purse aside again and took the turquoise one, unzipping it from its hanger. As I slipped into it, I glanced at him. "You must be quite familiar with the area, given your line of work."

A proud smile showcased dimples I hadn't noticed before. "Absolutely. The trails around here can be challenging, but that's what makes them exciting. I've spent a lot of time exploring every nook and cranny of these mountains."

I surveyed the coat in a nearby mirror and grinned. The man had excellent taste, and I hoped I wouldn't come to discover he was a murderer. "I love it."

His eyes sparkled. "If you decide to try skiing, you can rent skis at the lodge, but you might want to come back here for a good pair of gloves and a hat."

A salesman to the very end. "I'll definitely do that."

He carried the box of boots to the counter while I followed, struggling to shrug out of the coat while holding my oversized bag. "You're great at your job. It's nice to find someone so knowledgeable."

I passed the coat to him so he could scan the tag. "I heard you were interested in expanding your business, maybe even moving to a more central location in town. That must be exciting, considering the foot traffic and visibility."

Alex's expression shifted slightly. "Yes, expansion is always on my mind. A prime location can make a huge difference in this business."

I sensed an opening and took it. "I'm sure you've heard about what happened to that dress shop owner. It's so awful, but I'd guess her space might soon become available. It seems like it might be perfect for your needs."

His gaze grew more cautious. "It's an unfortunate situation, certainly. I wouldn't want to seem like I'm capitalizing on a tragedy, though."

I nodded, noting the careful way he navigated the topic. It was time to test the waters with our little spell. "The whole town's been talking about her murder, but it doesn't sound like the police have any solid leads. I don't suppose you were anywhere nearby that night and might have seen someone suspicious?"

Alex paused, staring at the price tag on the coat for several seconds. "I was leading a night hike. It was a last-minute thing, so there wasn't a formal sign-up."

The fact that he'd given me extra information about his hike would have made me suspicious, but that darned sickening feeling crept over me, too, luckily not as strong. I regarded him with new eyes, certain the expert outdoorsman was lying about his whereabouts the night Nan died.

I continued chatting as though I hadn't registered that information. "I only recently met Nan since my best friend is getting married and used her services. But I couldn't really get a feel for her. Was she a likable person?"

He shrugged. "I didn't know her well, either. To me, she was just another businessperson in town."

My stomach tightened at another lie, and I released a disturbed sigh. "I can't imagine who might do something like that to her. Can you? It's horrifying to say the least."

He released a slow breath and smiled. "I'm sure the police are working hard to figure it out. But I know she had issues with Taylor Hayes."

My eyebrows shot upward, and I was surprised nausea didn't accompany his statement. "Taylor? Why?"

He shrugged. "I'm not one for gossip, so let's just say I overheard someone talking about how Nan was trying to ruin Ms. Hayes, talking badly about her services to customers."

His information stunned me, and it seemed there might be some truth to it. After all, Taylor seemed to be struggling with something the last time I'd seen her. And there was that overdue notice that had been peeking out from a file on her desk.

Alex ended that topic by listing the total amount due for my purchases, and I nearly choked again. But after all my yapping and seeming excited about having ski-worthy wear, I would have been too embarrassed to put back the coat or boots. And I really did want to try skiing.

I dug my credit card out of my purse and handed it over, knowing I'd be dipping into my inheritance from Aunt Birdie as soon as my bill came due.

He finished the transaction and bagged my items, handing them over with a friendly look. "Here you go. You should stop by after your first ski day and let me know how you like it."

I mirrored his pleasant expression. "I'll be sure to do that. Thanks so much for your help today."

As I left the shop, the cool wind was a refreshing contrast to the intensity of our conversation and helped calm my nausea. I juggled my bags as I opened the door to Caden's truck and placed them and Kookie inside. She groaned as she looked at me. *I feel sick.*

I covered my stomach. "Me, too."

I don't like this spell very much.

I stroked her soft fur, hoping to soothe her. "Me, either. But I think it's helping us with the case, don't you?"

She gave me a weary look. *Only if Patricia and Alex both hurt Nan.*

As I headed for the driver's side, I considered her comment. Either the spell wasn't working, or they'd both been lying about something. But what?

I climbed inside the truck and started the engine. As I backed away, I noticed Alex staring out the window at us, and I wondered if he recognized Caden's truck. It wasn't as if most people in town didn't know the police chief and likely what he drove when off duty.

If so, Alex might have figured out I'd interrogated him. Which meant I needed to be more careful if I wanted to continue poking my nose into possible hornet's nests.

FIFTEEN

My thoughts darted in and out of the shadows in my mind as I drove to Taylor Hayes' house office the following afternoon. As I approached the front door of her pretty sage green home, I was hesitant to walk in without knocking, even though I'd arrived during business hours.

But that was most likely because she'd become a murder suspect in my mind and not just a wedding planner.

I steeled my nerves as I stepped inside and was greeted by the soft gray walls. Taylor's usually meticulous space was just as scattered as when I'd visited with Chloe not long before. The air seemed heavier now, and I wondered if the strain on the normally cool-headed Taylor had begun to crack her polished repute.

I rapped my knuckles on the side of her open office door, and she glanced up, her usual sharp, angular features softened by what seemed like weariness. She attempted a smile as she drew fingers through her long blond hair, but her demeanor was anything but cheerful. "Evie, what brings you here today?"

If only I could put everything out in the open and get an honest answer. Instead, I took a seat across from her and offered a friendly smile that I hoped would warm her demeanor. "I wanted to let you know about Chloe's wedding dress situation. She's found a website with some dresses she really likes, and I think she'll pick one from there. So, no worries about helping her find a seamstress."

Taylor's expression shifted to one of apology, a rare glimpse of vulnerability in her usually composed appearance. "I'm sorry I couldn't be of more help with finding a replacement dress. I've been waiting for a call back from a dressmaker about twenty miles out of town, but no luck."

Her words trailed off, and for a moment, she seemed lost in thought, her gaze fixed on a point beyond the cluttered desk. The disarray in her office spoke volumes, reflecting the turmoil that seemed to be unraveling her once impeccable professionalism.

I wondered if she'd even attempted to make calls on Chloe's behalf or if she'd been too caught up with whatever was going on in her life. Though what I really yearned to know was if her distress had anything to do with Nan's death. I leaned forward, my tone gentle yet firm. "Taylor, is everything okay? You don't seem like yourself."

She fought to smile as she smoothed over the papers on her desk as if that would put her world back in order. "I'm fine, Evie. Just a bit overwhelmed with work, that's all."

Her eyes betrayed the turmoil she was trying to conceal, and her expression tugged at my heart. "Hey, it's okay to admit if things aren't going well. We all face tough times."

The dam finally broke. Taylor's composure crumbled, and tears began to stream down her cheeks. She covered her face with her hands, her shoulders shaking with silent sobs. It was a startling and heart-wrenching sight, and for a moment, I didn't know what to do.

But the empathic side of me kicked in, and I grabbed several tissues for her, stuffing them into her hands. She blotted her eyes and tried to smile through her tears. "Look at me. I'm a blubbering mess and for no good reason at all."

I offered a sympathetic smile, encouraging her to continue. "I don't think people burst into tears for no reason. I'm a good listener, and maybe talking about it will help."

She took a deep breath, steadying herself. "You're the police chief's fiancée."

Her comment caused me to widen my eyes, but I played off my response with a lighthearted comeback. "That makes it sound like your troubles might be illegal."

Taylor dropped her shoulders and squeezed her eyes shut. "No. It's nothing like that. It's just that my business hasn't been doing well lately. I've had several big clients back out recently, and others haven't paid. Business has been down, and it couldn't have come at a worse time."

I couldn't help but wonder if her troubles had anything to do with Nanette Collingsworth.

She continued talking, her voice laced with frustration and fear. "I've been under so much pressure, trying to keep everything afloat. It feels like I'm losing control of the very thing I've worked so hard to build."

As I listened, I couldn't help but feel a pang of empathy for her situation, but that still didn't explain why she'd brought my relationship with Caden into our conversation. It might have been wrong of me to do so, but I took advantage of her vulnerability. "Taylor, I must ask, and please know it's only out of concern. Do your business troubles have anything to do with Nanette's death?"

Taylor's eyes widened slightly at the question, and she quickly composed herself, shaking her head. "No, no. Of course not. My issues are purely business-related. Nanette's death was a shock to us all, but it has nothing to do with my current situation."

Even though I only had residual bits of the spell in my system, her admission left me queasy, and my intuition whispered that there was more to her story. There had to be a way to force her to talk, and it seemed that a white lie of my own might be the answer. "Taylor, I'm not sure you're aware, but I'm part of the local coven in town."

Her eyes rounded into wide ovals. "You're a witch?"

I nodded sagely. "I am. And I'll be honest with you." I paused to draw the jasper necklace that connected me to Aunt Birdie from beneath my shirt. "See this stone? It grows hot when someone lies. And right now, it's *very* warm."

Taylor grasped at her neck, her remaining composure faltering. "You... You think I'm lying?"

I maintained my serious demeanor. "I know that you are. I can sense when things aren't as they seem. Is that why you're worried that I'm dating Caden? Because I'll tell him what I learn? Please, Taylor, if you're holding something back, especially regarding Nanette, now is the time to share it. The longer you hold onto your lies, the worse your life will become. And you know the police will figure things out."

The room was thick with uneasiness, the air charged with the weight of my deception and the uncertainty of Taylor's next words. It was a risky move, but one I hoped would bring us closer to the truth. And just to be on the safe side, I was fully prepared to magically shove her to the ground if she tried to attack or run.

Taylor hesitated, her eyes flickering with a mix of emotions. The revelation that I was a witch seemed to have unsettled her, and she appeared to be wrestling with an internal struggle. Finally, with a deep sigh, she began to speak, her voice holding a hint of sadness.

"You know, my relationship with Nanette wasn't always strained. We used to be friends, but then things changed."

Tingles raced up my arms as I prepared to act. "Why?"

She gave me a sad shrug. "I'm not sure. I can only guess, but I wonder if it's because of the day I stopped by her dress shop unannounced. I walked in on Nanette and Patricia's husband, Raul, standing... unusually close. It was intimate. At least it seemed that way to me. They immediately jumped apart when they saw me, and Patricia hastily explained she was taking his measurements. Which could have been the truth. But the whole scene felt off."

Taylor's gaze drifted away, lost in the memory. "I didn't actually see anything incriminating, but it made me wonder. Could Patricia's accusations have some truth to them? After that incident, Nanette became cold toward me. It was as if I had seen something I wasn't supposed to."

She flicked her gaze to me, her expression a mixture of confusion and hurt. "Then, things started going downhill for my business. One of my clients mentioned that Nan had been spreading rumors about me, saying I couldn't be trusted. It felt like she was trying to sabotage my business. I don't know if that was her way of threatening me to keep quiet or what."

The weight of her words hung heavily in the room, and I scooted to the edge of my chair and leaned in.

"So, what happened that night? Did she come at you? Did she force you to defend yourself?"

The color drained from her face. "*What?* No. Oh, my god, Evie. *I didn't kill Nan.* I was at home that night. Just me and my cats, binge-watching a crime drama. Nan was the one with the grudge. *Not me.*"

Her non-confession surprised me. But I had to admit my stomach didn't twist even the tiniest bit. I covered my mouth in embarrassment. "Oh, wow. I feel like a fool. I hope you can forgive me for jumping to conclusions. It just really sounded like you were confessing."

She stared at me, blinking several times. "I don't even know what to say. Is my reputation around town that bad? Is that why I'm losing clients?"

I quickly waved my hands between us. "Not even. I think you have a great reputation. I know Chloe loves working with you. In fact, I'll be getting married sometime soon, and I'd love it if you could help me, too."

The hard set of her shoulders softened, and her eyes grew moist again. "Everything has been such a mess since the day I walked in on them. I know this is awful to say, but I'd hoped after Nan's death, things would get better for me." She tucked in her lips, her expression turning horrified as if I might think she was confessing again.

I lifted a hand to calm her. "I believe you, Taylor. There's nothing wrong with wanting someone out of your life if they make things harder." I paused to release a soft chuckle. "As long as you don't kill them."

She grimaced and nodded carefully. "Right."

I reached forward to pat her hand. "Thank you for being open with me. Maybe now that you're not wondering if everyone thinks you're guilty, you can concentrate on your business again."

"Will you tell Caden that you believe me?"

I gave her a resolute nod. "I will. And I'll be sure to talk up your business, telling everyone how helpful you've been to Chloe."

Taylor nodded, a faint smile gracing her lips. "Thank you, Evie. I appreciate your understanding, and I'm glad Chloe's no longer worried about finding her dress."

As I stood to leave, I sensed a shift in the atmosphere. The tension had dissipated, replaced by a sense of ease.

Outside, I took a moment to gather my thoughts. The conversation had revealed much about the dynamics between Taylor, Nanette, and Patricia, painting a picture of entangled personal and professional relationships.

As I walked away, my mind turned to Raul Lane, Patricia's husband. Taylor's account of the intimate encounter between him and Nan, and the subsequent fallout, was a lead that couldn't be ignored. I made a mental note to discuss this with Caden, to ask him to delve deeper into Raul's alibi, to see if he could shed more light on the man's involvement.

SIXTEEN

The following afternoon, I left the bakery early to go to Nan's funeral. Valerie hadn't minded. In fact, she'd been happy that I could represent both of us since she needed to stay and mind the store.

With the cemetery not being far from where I lived, I stopped by my house for a few minutes to change. As I slipped on a pair of black flats that matched my flowing black skirt, I glanced down at Kookie who sat near my feet watching me. "I'm headed to a funeral," I said, knowing she'd be interested.

Kookie cocked her cute orange and black head. *What's that?*

"It's where we honor a person who's no longer living."

She gave me a look of understanding. *Nan.*

I finished my shoe and scooped her up, holding her close to my face. "That's right. Most funerals are sad occasions where people cry a lot. I'm not looking forward to going."

But you need to.

I shrugged. "It feels like I do. I think solving the mystery of Nan's murder is the best way to honor her life, don't you? She deserves to rest in peace."

Can I come with you? I promise to stay in your purse and behave.

Her question warmed my heart. "Yes, you can come."

After my parents' deaths, I'd steered clear of most funerals, so having Kookie to hug would be a comfort to me. "And there's no reason to hide you today. We'll be outside, and you're as welcome as anyone else."

Kookie's happiness filtered into me, bolstering me more.

The gray sky above seemed to reflect the somber mood of the occasion as I parked Caden's truck several minutes later and turned to Kookie. "Let's skip the truth-telling spell today. It always leaves us feeling sick, and this isn't the place for it."

But we need to know the truth, Evie. This is important.

Her bright eyes held determination, and I couldn't help but feel a swell of pride. I studied her for a moment, wanting to argue. But I couldn't. "You're right. If it will help Nan, we should do it."

I murmured the incantation discreetly, preparing us for whatever truths or lies we might encounter. The sensation of magic gathered around us, and I climbed out with Kookie tucked against me.

The solemnity of the cemetery enveloped us as we passed through the wrought iron gates, and I headed toward the gathering off to the side. The rows of tombstones stood like silent sentinels, guarding the memories of those who rested beneath them. And now there would be one more.

We were late arriving, and the funeral service had already begun, so I chose to stay at the back of the gathered mourners, not wanting to intrude upon the intimate grief of those closest to Nan. Kookie, nestled quietly against me, seemed to understand the gravity of the moment.

From our vantage point, I could see the mourners' bowed heads and hear the soft cadence of the eulogy, a tribute to a life that had ended too soon. The air was thick with sorrow; each person lost in their own reflections and memories of Nanette Collingsworth.

My gaze drifted across the crowd, observing the faces of those who had come to pay their respects. Among them, I noticed the same dark-haired man that I'd seen in the photo on Patricia's desk. Raul Lane stood alone, his posture betraying a deep sense of loss. His presence here, without Patricia, was notable, and his demeanor added more credence to my emerging suspicions that he *had* been in a relationship with Nan.

I was also surprised to see Taylor and Alex West in attendance. Both stood apart from the main group, their presence somewhat unexpected. Alex's rugged features were set in a somber expression, a sharp contrast to his usual confident demeanor. And Taylor appeared visibly shaken, her eyes red-rimmed from crying.

Their motives for coming baffled me. Maybe it was Taylor's way of putting things behind her, but what about Alex? Was his presence a show of respect, or was there something more to it?

As the eulogy ended and the mourners began to disperse, my attention remained fixed on Raul Lane. His reaction to the service was more profound than I had anticipated. Tears streamed down his face unabashedly, his body occasionally shuddering with sobs. It was a display of raw grief that seemed to cut through the formalities of the funeral.

Alex was one of the first to leave, and I hurried to place myself in his path, hoping for a quick conversation. His head was down as he strode toward me, but as he neared, he looked up. Immediate wariness appeared in his eyes.

I lifted my hand in greeting and spoke softly. "Hey, Alex. I'm surprised to see you here since you didn't know Nan well."

Before I could continue, he firmly shook his head. "Sorry, Evie. I don't have time to chat right now. Drop by the shop sometime."

With that, he left me open-mouthed as I watched him hurry away.

Kookie squirmed against me. *He's up to something.*

"It sure seems that way," I muttered. But I wasn't letting my next victim off the hook so easily.

As the crowd began to thin, I set my sights on Raul. His emotional state at the funeral was intriguing and heartbreaking at the same time. There must have been more to their relationship, and he obviously no longer cared who knew it.

I turned to Kookie. We both nodded at each other with firm resolve, and I headed toward the grieving man.

Raul stood a solitary figure against the backdrop of Nanette's grave, the scent of fresh earth and wilting flowers mingling in the air. His shoulders were hunched, bearing the weight of unspoken sorrow.

His genuine pain tugged at my heart, and I spoke in a soft voice. "Mr. Lane, I'm so sorry for your loss. I didn't realize you and Nan were so close."

Raul turned to me, a flicker of confusion crossing his face before it settled back into a mask of grief. "Thank you. Nanette was a special person. It's a terrible loss for the whole town now that she'll no longer be around to share her smiles and beautiful creations."

I could hear the tremble in his voice, see the struggle to maintain his composure. His pain was palpable, filling the space between us with a tangible ache. As awful as Nan might have been, and as twisted as her relationships were, I was glad she had at least one person who cared deeply for her.

His openness encouraged me, and I cautiously ventured further. "I can see how much she meant to you, letting me know the rumors I've heard are outright lies."

He sniffed as a worried look crossed his face. "Rumors?"

I grimaced as though it pained me to tell him, which it did. "There's been some talk about your involvement in her murder. But seeing you here, so affected by her passing, it's hard to reconcile that with the gossip."

Raul's reaction was immediate and visceral. His face drained of color, and he looked at me with a mixture of hurt and disbelief. "*Involved in her murder?* How could people think that? I would never harm Nanette."

His denial was fervent, yet beneath it, I sensed a flicker of something unspoken. Along with that, the churning in my gut told me he lied. It seemed Raul had something to do with Nan's death, and he was hiding it.

I was determined to find out exactly what. "I'm sorry to bring it up," I continued, maintaining a sympathetic tone. "It's just that with everything that's been happening, it's hard to know what to believe."

Kookie, sensing the intensity of the moment, lifted her paw to my chest, her touch and silent vigilance a comfort.

Raul seemed to wrestle with his thoughts for a moment before he swallowed and composed himself. Though there was nothing he could do about those red-rimmed eyes. "I understand people talk, but I assure you, my relationship with Nanette was nothing but friendly. The idea that I could be involved in her death is... It's just unthinkable."

He'd closed off his emotions, and I wished I'd learned more before he did. Still, I had no choice but to nod, assuring him that I understood. After a few more words of condolence, I excused myself, leaving Raul to his mourning.

As I walked away, my mind was abuzz with questions and theories. When I was far enough away from him, I lifted my kitty closer to my face. "Lying for sure, right?"

Kookie gave me a matter-of-fact nod.

I narrowed my gaze in suspicion. "I believe I got the first sensation right when I asked about his involvement with her death."

She nosed my chin, hers feeling mildly warm. *Yes.*

I released a sigh of satisfaction as I studied her to make sure she was okay. "This was our most successful use of the spell, wouldn't you say?"

Her eyes widened in alarm, and she pushed her paws against my chest. Before I could ask what was wrong, she vomited all over the front of my coat. I glanced down in horror as she turned her head and wretched again. My own stomach was a tangled mess, and the scent of her puke made me gag.

Luckily, I managed to hold things together until we reached Caden's truck. "Deep breaths of fresh air, if you can." I took my own advice and filled my lungs, accepting the respite that helped to calm my stomach.

Kookie lowered her ears as I placed her on the seat, her eyes full of apology. *I'm sorry, Evie.*

I reassured her with a shake of my head as I removed my coat and rolled it to contain the mess. "Don't be sorry. It's the spell, not you. I think maybe we should retire that one and see if we can find another. What do you say?"

She nodded her head before resting it on the seat. *I want to go home and sleep.*

I felt the same way. We needed to rest and refresh. Everything else could wait.

SEVENTEEN

The day was waning into a quiet evening as I made my way to Chloe's place. We had planned a casual catch-up, a brief respite from the whirlwind of events that had been consuming our days, and I wanted to fill her in on what I learned from Taylor. As I approached her cozy home, huddled among a row of charming townhomes, something immediately felt amiss.

The front door, usually securely closed, was ajar, leaving me with a sense of unease. I hurried toward it, and the faint murmur of voices drifting out didn't help matters. I edged closer, my instincts as both a friend and a witch kicking in.

Through the slightly open door, the scene before me was unexpected and charged with emotion. Chloe's ex-boyfriend Brandon stood in the middle of the living room, his posture tense, his voice laced with desperation. His hair seemed shaggier than the last time I'd seen him, and he might have been wearing the same shirt that he had then, too.

Brandon spoke, emphatically gesturing with his hands. "Chloe, you can't marry him. You know we're meant to be together." His intense eyes brimmed with unshed tears, reflecting a turmoil that seemed to run deep.

I hesitated at the threshold, torn between intervening and respecting Chloe's privacy. Brandon's demeanor was fevered, but he didn't currently strike me as dangerous. Chloe had obviously opened the door to him, and although she sat on the couch looking visibly upset, she didn't seem afraid.

"Brandon, we've been over this," she said in a firm voice tinged with sadness. "Please. *Listen to me.* I care about you, but my future is with Riley. We had our chance, and it didn't work. I believe that was for a reason. The most I can offer you is friendship."

It was clear she was struggling, caught between her past with Brandon and her commitment to Riley, but I knew where her heart resided.

Brandon clenched and unclenched his hands as he paced the room, making me more nervous as his words spilled out in a torrent of emotion. "I don't think so. I think I made a huge mistake, and Riley capitalized on it. I always intended to come back, Chloe. How can you just walk away from what we had?"

Obviously, their past relationship still held a powerful grip on him, but Chloe responded in a gentle but unwavering voice, showing her resolve.

As I stood there, a silent observer, I weighed my options. Chloe wasn't asking him to leave, and there was a part of me that felt this was a conversation they needed to have. Yet, another part of me was ready to step in if the situation escalated.

Chloe stood, maintaining her composure despite the emotional onslaught, and she tried again. "Brandon, what we had was important to me, but it's part of my past. Riley is my future. I'm sorry, but you need to accept that."

Brandon's face contorted with disbelief. "How can you be so sure? How can you just erase everything we had? Shouldn't we at least try?" His plea was heartfelt, and I found his raw display of vulnerability painful to witness.

Chloe's expression softened with concern as she watched him, her words laced with a mix of worry and sincerity. "Brandon, I'm worried about you. You've always been so strong, so sure of yourself. But now, I can't help but wonder if you've lost your edge."

Brandon's eyes widened, a flicker of confusion crossing his face. "What do you mean?"

Chloe sighed and took a cautious step backward. "You wouldn't do something crazy to try and stop my wedding, would you?"

I sucked in a surprised breath, shocked she'd taken the conversation in that direction when she was alone with him.

The accusation hung in the air, heavy and charged with implications. Brandon paled, his body going rigid. "Spell it out, Chloe. What is it you think I've done?"

She tilted her head, offering him the gentle, kind smile she often used. "I mean, I hope you haven't taken things too far in trying to stop my wedding. The thought that you might have tried to ruin my dress... And what if doing so had led to something worse?" Her last words came out in a whisper. "What if you had something to do with Nan's death?"

It was at this moment that I knew I had to intervene. The conversation was teetering on the edge of a dangerous precipice, and if Brandon was indeed unhinged, Chloe's accusation could push him over.

I knocked sharply on the door to alert them before I stepped into the room. "Hi, Chloe." I pretended to be surprised to see her old boyfriend. "Oh, hey Brandon. I didn't expect to find you here."

He looked from me to Chloe, his expression a turmoil of hurt and confusion, and I hoped he'd soon realize he had lost her forever. "I was actually just leaving," he said to me, and then turned to my friend, speaking in a lowered voice filled with anguish. "I can't believe you'd think I could do something like that. Just because I was with Nan not long before she was killed and just because I don't want you to get married doesn't mean I had anything to do with it."

I wasn't shocked to hear that he'd been with Nan sometime before her death since Caden had told me of the dinner jacket he'd sold back to Nan, but I was surprised that Brandon had brought it up.

He ran a hand through his hair, a gesture of exasperation and despair. "Okay, I did ask if she could stall on your dress. But she refused, and when I left her, she was alive and well. If you don't believe me, ask Whitney. I bumped into her right after I left Nan's shop. We ended up going out for ice cream sundaes to catch up."

Chloe, still processing Brandon's admission, remained silent, her expression slowly turning to fear. The room was thick with tension, the revelation hanging heavily between us.

I stepped forward, addressing Brandon with a calm yet firm tone. "You've said what you came to say, and I think you should go."

Brandon looked defeated, the fight draining out of him. "I know, I know. I just... I never meant for any of this to happen." He strode to the door and glanced back one last time. "I love you, Chloe."

With that, he was gone, leaving a cold chill behind. I took my friend's hand and led her to the couch where we both sat, me concerned and her looking shell-shocked as she gazed across the room and whispered. "Never in a million years did I think he'd do something like this."

She focused on me. "You believe him, right? That he didn't hurt Nan?"

I blew out a frustrated breath. "I don't know. Maybe? He seemed sincere with everything else he said. I didn't get the sense he was hiding anything, did you?"

Chloe lifted her hands into the air and let them drop. "I don't know anything at this point. Everything is just a confused mess."

I widened my eyes. "You're not having second thoughts about marrying Riley, are you?"

She focused on me with a stern look, her words fierce. "No. I love him with all my heart."

I nodded in relief. I knew Riley was the right man for her. "Chloe," I said softly. "Why did you let Brandon into your house? That could have been dangerous."

She sighed, a weary expression crossing her face. "I know. But I felt I needed to clear things up with him once and for all. Before I move forward with Riley, I wanted to make sure there were no loose ends with my past."

Her words resonated with a sense of closure and responsibility. It was clear that Chloe was trying to navigate her past and present with care, even if it meant facing uncomfortable situations. But that was my friend, a woman with a good and kind heart.

The front door burst open, startling both of us, and Riley, appearing as if he'd come straight from an intense workout at the gym, glanced between us with a wild look in his eyes. "Is everything okay?"

Chloe stood up, walking over to him. "Thanks for coming home. Everything's okay. Brandon was here.

He wanted to talk about us... about the wedding." She glanced at me before continuing. "I wasn't completely reckless, Evie. I knew you'd be coming, and I did text Riley, giving me and Brandon just enough time to talk."

Riley's expression softened as he wrapped his arms around Chloe, offering her a comforting embrace. "I wished you'd waited until I was here, but I'm just glad you're safe," he said, his voice filled with relief.

A sense of reassurance washed over me. Chloe had handled the situation with more foresight than I had given her credit for. "I'll leave you two to talk," I said, standing up. "Message me later."

With a final nod to them both, I made my way to the door. The day's events had given me much to think about, and I knew my next stop had to be Caden's house. I didn't think Brandon would confess to asking Nan to stall on Chloe's wedding dress if he was guilty, but one never knew.

EIGHTEEN

E ven though I had a key to Caden's charming log cabin, I still let him know I was on my way. But when I stepped inside the cozy ambiance of his living room, a wave of surprise washed over me. There, curled up comfortably on his couch, was Kookie.

My little familiar had never wandered off on her own before, and seeing her here, in Caden's living room, was both startling and endearing. "What's little Miss Mischief doing here?"

Caden greeted me with a warm smile, a hint of amusement in his eyes. "Seems like you have a little adventurer on your hands. She showed up on my porch a while ago, meowing to be let in."

As I approached, Kookie opened her bright eyes and quickly blinked away all traces of sleep. *I'm big enough to go places by myself. Mochi wouldn't play, and I wanted to see Caden.*

Her words brought a smile to my face, even though I disagreed with her running around by herself. "Well,

I'm glad you like him," I replied, both amused and slightly bewildered by her newfound adventurous spirit.

Caden winked at me. "She's been giving me a lot of sweet kitty kisses."

I arched my brow at Kookie. "Trying to steal my man, huh?"

She stood, turned in a circle, and curled into a ball again. *He's mine, too, you know.*

Who was I to argue with that?

I sat next to her and tugged her onto my lap, stroking her soft fur as she purred, obviously content. Caden sat beside me, and I focused on him. "I just came from Chloe's, and you'll never guess who I found there."

He frowned. "Did Riley crash your party?"

"Brandon showed up."

He stiffened. *"He what?"*

I nodded, giving him a look that said I wholeheartedly agreed with his reaction. "He was begging Chloe to take him back, to give them one more chance. It was more than just a simple case of heartbreak or jealousy. His emotions were all over the place, almost unhinged."

I paused, recalling the scene. "He admitted to being with Nan just before she was murdered, which you knew. But I bet he didn't tell you that he tried to convince Nan to stall on Chloe's dress."

His eyebrows shot upward. *"He what?"*

I pursed my lips before I continued. "Part of me thinks he's a wounded soul, but the rest of me is worried about what he might do next."

He furrowed his brows in concern. "Same. Do you think I should put a detail on Chloe?"

I shrugged as worry knotted my stomach. "Maybe. Riley came home, so she's fine right now. But him asking Nan to stall? That's crossing a line, if you ask me."

Caden wrapped his arm around me and tugged me close. "Definitely. We'd mostly excluded him from the investigation since his story checked out initially, but this new behavior is concerning. Don't worry. We'll protect Chloe."

His words comforted me, and I leaned into him. "I wanted to talk to you about Raul Lane, too. I saw him at Nan's funeral, and he was an emotional wreck, too."

He turned to me with an interested look. "Is that so? I can't imagine why he'd show after all the accusations Patricia's made about the two of them."

I nodded, the image of Raul at the funeral still vivid in my mind. "That's what I thought, too. But he wasn't hiding his emotions at all. He was visibly upset, more than I would have expected, and it was troubling to see. His grief seemed genuine, but given everything we've heard, it makes me curious about the true nature of their relationship."

I paused, gathering my thoughts. "Kookie and I spoke to him afterward. We used the truth-telling spell, and we sensed he was lying when I brought up the rumors of his involvement with Nan's death."

Kookie meowed, confirming my statement, and then groaned.

Caden turned to her with a look of worry. "You got sick again?"

She nodded, giving him a pitiful look.

I sighed. "She puked all over me. But it's my fault. I take full responsibility, and Kookie and I agree that we're not going to use that spell any longer."

Caden chuckled softly before he leaned back, his expression thoughtful. "So, Raul was lying about Nan, too?"

I pressed on, wanting him to understand the depth of my concern. "Tell me again about his alibi? Is it airtight? Was there proof he was with his brother at the time of the murder?"

He gave me a half shrug. "His brother vouched for him, but we didn't find any independent verification of his whereabouts. It seems it's something we need to revisit, especially considering this new information."

The conversation deepened my unease about Raul Lane, and I wasn't sure who bothered me the most. Him or Brandon. Both were highly suspicious in my book. For now, I'd done what I could with both avenues, and it seemed best to let Caden intervene.

As we sat together, both lost in our thoughts, my phone vibrated with a new message. Seeing that it was from Chloe, I quickly opened it to find her text saying, *This is the one!*

I sucked in an excited breath as I tapped the link. "I think Chloe's found her dress. Want to see?"

The screen displayed a stunning wedding dress from the Weddings by Design website. She'd chosen one that was elegant and sophisticated with lots of fluttery lace in a full princess ball gown style. "It's perfect for Chloe, don't you think?"

He smiled. "Yep. Seems perfect. She'll be a beautiful bride." He paused to lean over and kiss my head. "But not as beautiful as you."

I snorted, pretending I didn't love his comment. "You know, Whitney might not have been the best friend she claims to be, but she may have just saved the day with this wedding dress suggestion."

I scrolled through the images, each showcasing the dress's exquisite details. I couldn't wait to see Chloe in it. "Whitney's company did marketing for Weddings by Design, so I guess that gave her great insight into what they have." I tapped on the home page and found the picture of Whitney with the owner. "See? Whitney's even on their website."

Caden leaned closer, his eyes scanning the image. "That's nice. I'm glad it's helped Chloe."

I nodded, still looking at the phone. "It's a bit of a silver lining, given everything that's happened."

Caden slipped the phone from my hands and examined the picture closer. "Are you sure Whitney claimed to be working for an external marketing firm, because it looks like she's wearing an employee badge here."

I frowned and snatched my phone back, squinting for a better look. Sure enough, I could see a swirling design on her badge that matched the one in the website's header. I snorted in disbelief. "I wonder if she's a perpetual liar, and if she can't help herself, because I can't see any reason why she wouldn't say she worked for them if she did. Unless she needs to make herself seem more important. The thing is, I don't think anyone around here cares what she's doing as long as she's happy, you know?"

Caden nodded, but his expression remained thoughtful. "I'll be honest, Evie. Her inconsistencies are starting to concern me. If she's fabricating details about her employment, what else might she be hiding? And why?"

I sighed, feeling a tangle of emotions. "I want to believe she's just trying to help, and it's not like her lies have hurt anyone."

He shrugged. "I don't know. She works in the wedding dress business, and Chloe's dress designer was murdered. That's a connection."

I scoffed. "A vague one. You're too skeptical for your own good. Besides, I clearly heard Whitney tell Betty at the giftshop that she'd just arrived in town that morning, which was the day *after* the murder, so..."

I shot him a doubtful look. "I think Raul Lane comes across as much more suspicious."

Caden turned and pulled me across his lap with a teasing look in his eyes. "Too skeptical? You're as bad as me."

I grinned. "Guilty as charged."

He leaned close to kiss me just as another memory popped into my head. I lifted a hand to stop him, and he ended up planting his lips on my palm. I wrinkled my nose in apology at his look of disappointment. "Sorry. But something's not right."

"Are you kidding me?" he growled.

I ignored his playful threat. "Listen to this. At Chloe's tonight, Brandon said he and Whitney had gone for ice cream sundaes after he left Nan's shop. How could that happen if Whitney wasn't in town until the next day?"

Caden's demeanor shifted, his detective instincts clearly engaged. "That's very interesting. If Whitney was indeed in town that night, then why lie to Betty? And if she wasn't, then Brandon's lying."

A chill ran down my spine as the implications of their contradictions sank in. "Does that mean one of them is the murderer?" I whispered.

He cocked his head. "Maybe. Maybe not. But the sooner we get answers, the better. If I had direct evidence tying them to the crime, I'd have them brought to the station right now, but this will have to wait until morning."

I clamped my hand on my forehead. "Good luck. Seriously, is there anyone around here who doesn't lie or keep secrets?"

He gave me an odd look and then chuckled. "Not from what I've seen."

NINETEEN

Valerie and I were on pins and needles in the bakery the next morning after I told her Caden would soon interview Brandon and Whitney. Our mixers whirred, sending scents of vanilla and sugar into the air as the minutes dragged by, until she finally turned to me and shook her head. "I don't know, Evie. I really can't believe Nan's murderer is someone Chloe was close to. It seems so unreal."

I snorted. "Well, we know she loved Brandon, but was she really that close to Whitney? I think that woman speaks more lies than truths."

Valerie cocked her head. "Yeah, but still. To kill Nan? Why would she?"

I had to admit that bothered me, too. The evidence wasn't strong enough.

When my phone buzzed, we both jumped. I quickly wiped my hands and slipped it from my apron pocket. When I spotted Caden's name on the screen, I gave

Valerie a quick nod and answered the call. "How did it go?"

Caden released a long sigh. "Couldn't get Whitney to deviate from her story, even when I told her someone else's account of that evening varied from hers. She looked me straight in the eye and swore by what she said."

I blew out a slow, frustrated breath. "What about Brandon?"

"Haven't been able to locate him this morning. I have multiple officers looking for him."

A chill cracked over my head and slithered to my feet. "I don't like that."

His voice was full of concern when he spoke. "Me, either. But let's not get ahead of ourselves. He could be innocent. Chloe's at work and should be safe while we look for him."

I glanced at her mom, knowing this would upset her, too. "Okay. Keep me updated." I hung up the phone and turned to Valerie. "They're looking for Brandon."

Her eyes widened in alarm. "They can't find him?"

I waved my hands between us, hoping to calm her. "It's not like he's on the run. I'm guessing he wasn't at home when they stopped in. He could be having breakfast at the Gooseberry Café. Or could be out fishing or hiking."

Her frown told me I hadn't convinced her, so I continued. "I feel the same way. It's unsettling, and I want to be with Chloe to make sure she's okay."

My boss stared at me for a long moment before she jerked on her apron's tie, releasing it, and pulled it over her head. I gaped at her. "What are you doing?"

"I'm going with you."

I blinked, trying to process her answer. Was I going somewhere?

She tossed her apron into the hamper and grabbed her coat. "What are you waiting for? You want to go check on her, and so do I."

I tugged on my apron strings, surprised by her strong reaction. "We could probably call and check on her."

Valerie placed both hands on her hips. "If my daughter's life might be at stake, I'm not calling. I'm going to kidnap her and bring her back here where it's safe. Are you coming or not?"

I pulled the apron over my head and hurried for my coat. "Absolutely."

Once we were in my boss's car, she wasted no time starting the engine and throwing the car into reverse. Her tires squealed when she pulled out of the parking lot behind the bakery and turned toward Main Street, coming to a quick halt at the stop sign.

Guilt rolled through me from the amount of fear radiating from her, because I knew my reactions had heightened it. I placed a comforting hand on her arm as she signaled to turn. "It's going to be okay. I'm sure Chloe's fine."

Her green eyes flashed me a warning, and I knew better than to stop a mom from doing what she could to protect her child.

Valerie pulled onto Main Street, going faster than she should, heading for the boutique clothing store where Chloe worked. We hadn't gone more than a block when a small red car came zooming toward us on the other side of the street, also speeding. I stared at the driver, shocked when I spotted Whitney with her hands gripping the top of the steering wheel as she leaned toward her windshield. The determined, fearful look on her face was like a cold slap of water.

"Valerie. *Stop the car.*"

She came to a screeching halt in the middle of the road, and I was glad no one was right behind us or they might have hit us. "That was Whitney," I said, sounding breathless and pointing in the opposite direction. "She's scared, and she's running."

Valerie's nostrils flared. "Like hell she is."

The woman turned her car around so fast that I had to hold on or be tossed in my seat. She floored it, bouncing my head off the headrest. I wouldn't have expected the sedan to be so powerful, but it gained speed in no time.

My heart raced wildly as I jerked the phone from my pocket and called Caden. "It's Whitney," I practically yelled, mindlessly thinking I needed to be heard over the roaring engine. "She's trying to leave town." I took a quick breath. "I'm with Valerie, and we're chasing her."

"What?" The volume of Caden's exclamation stunned me. "Stop. Let me send officers after her."

I shifted a sideways glance at my boss, noting her wild eyes and determination. "I... I don't think that's going to happen. Just hurry. We're headed south on Main. Whitney's driving a little red car."

"Evie," Caden warned, and I lowered my phone. I wouldn't hang up in case we needed him, but arguing with him or trying to cajole Valerie would only distract me, and I needed all my senses at the moment.

Valerie thrust a finger forward. *"She's there.* I see her."

Before I could spot Whitney's car, an old blue truck pulled out right in front of us, and I tensed, expecting Valerie to slam on the brakes or send us skidding toward a row of green garbage cans. But she smoothly went around that sucker like she was a highly trained racecar driver, leaving my mouth hanging open.

We slowly gained ground on Whitney, but I had no idea how Valerie intended to make her stop. I certainly hoped she wasn't planning to run her off the road. That might kill us all.

Calm thinking was called for, and I surveyed our surroundings as we whizzed past, getting ever closer to the canyon at the edge of town. I needed a way to stop Whitney and searched for ideas. I remembered Birdie causing a torrential downpour when she wanted me to remain in Honeysuckle Springs. But I had a feeling that wouldn't slow either woman.

Perhaps I could conjure a wind that would force Whitney off the road. As I considered that option, the sight of another green garbage can caught my attention as we drove past, adding to the idea. It was garbage day, and I had a row of mostly harmless weapons at my disposal.

"I'm going to try to stop her," I yelled, caught up in the excitement. "So be careful. Stuff is going to fly into the road."

The spell rolled off my tongue in a rapid whisper. "Gods of the Four Winds, come out to play. Swirl all around us today. I will need more than a gentle breeze. Give me all you've got, if you please."

Energy roared through me, and I focused the core of my power on the green can ahead. It rocked before it hurled itself onto the road, spilling its contents on the asphalt before the gusts sent papers and bags flying. Whitney tapped her brakes, trying to navigate the debris, and Valerie cried out. "It's working!"

Of course, we also had to dodge random discarded items, but at least it caused both drivers to reduce their speeds, making me feel much better.

"Do another one," Valerie hollered.

So I did. The next house along the highway had two cans available. I waited until Whitney's car was almost there and sent them flying. She slammed on her brakes this time, almost barreling headfirst into one of them before she over-corrected. Her car careened to the other side, hitting the dirt alongside the pavement, and spun.

Dust swirled around her car as ours came to a jolting halt next to her.

Valerie jumped out of her sedan so fast that she scared me. I knew she was protective of Chloe, but I guess I hadn't realized the depth of it. I quickly caught up to her, grabbing her arm and pulling her to a stop. "Let me handle this. I can use my magic to detain her."

Valerie seemed uncertain, but she let me take the lead as Whitney opened her door and stepped out. The guilty woman looked at us with wide-eyed relief as she glanced around. "Thank you so much for stopping to help me. Was that... was that a mini tornado or what?"

Or what, I thought as I stepped forward. I glanced at her suitcases in the backseat and then focused on her. "Where are you going in such a hurry?"

My question seemed to shock her. "What do you mean? Didn't you see what just happened?"

I took another step closer and spoke in a low voice. "I *caused* what just happened, and I'll ask again. Where do you think you're going? Because it looks an awful lot like you're running from the law."

The color drained from her face, and she jerked her gaze to her car, likely assessing her chances of escaping.

I continued my interrogation. "I know you were questioned this morning about Nan's death, and now here you are, rushing out of town. Seems a little suspicious to me."

She swallowed as terror reflected in her eyes. "What are you talking about, Evie? I'm not running. I was unexpectedly called back to work."

I snorted. "Is that right? Would that be your marketing job or Weddings by Design job? Because I know you lied about where you work."

Whitney blinked, and I was certain her mind was racing, searching for the next lie. "I don't know what this is all about, Evie. Why are you saying these things?"

Valerie growled, and I put out an arm to stop her from going after Whitney. I narrowed my eyes, convinced we'd found the murderer. "The real question is, why did you kill Nan? Not that I can trust what you say because you've pretty much lied about everything else."

"Why?" Valerie pleaded. "You say you're Chloe's best friend. Why would you hurt her this way?"

My boss must have gotten to her, because Whitney's demeanor shifted significantly. "I wasn't trying to hurt Chloe. She was one of the nicest people to me while I was growing up."

I cocked my head. "But you've dragged her right into the middle of this. You killed Nan while she was wearing Chloe's wedding dress."

She opened her mouth and closed it several times before she answered. "I tried to help her find a new one. My company has some of the prettiest dresses out there."

I was certain Whitney was guilty, but I still couldn't figure her out. Before I could question her further, the old blue truck that had pulled out in front of Valerie slowly drove up alongside us. I recognized one of the old lumberjacks in town, Frederic Farber, as he lowered his window and peered at us. "Everything okay here?"

Valerie, with her unflappable manners, gave him a kind smile. "Thanks for stopping, but we're just fine. A minor incident. Why don't you stop in at the bakery next week for a free cookie? I haven't seen your handsome face in a while."

He gave her a crooked grin and nodded. "Sure thing, Miss Valerie. I'd love that."

She smiled and waved him on his way. He cranked up the window on his truck, gripped the wheel, and it crept forward.

I shifted my full gaze to Whitney, ready to get back to business. "Then why Nan?"

The break in our conversation must have bolstered her, because she smiled and shook her head. "I don't know what you're talking about."

But the distant sound of sirens quickly erased her fake expression. "It's too late, Whitney. The police are on to your tactics. You won't be able to lie your way out of this one, so just tell us. Why Nan? What did she do to you to bring about such anger?"

Her lip quivered as darkness filled her eyes. "I didn't mean to kill her. It was an accident, okay? I only stopped at her shop to check out the competition. But when I noticed the sparsity of her available collection and asked how long it took her to make a wedding dress, I knew she was doomed to fail."

She dropped her gaze to the side as if reevaluating what she'd said. "I probably shouldn't have told her so. But really, I was doing her a favor, giving her a chance to get things in order before she went out of business. With us moving into the neighboring town, it was only a matter of time."

I switched to a look of understanding, encouraging her to continue. "I get that. Things sometimes happen that we can't predict. What did Nan say when you told her that?"

Whitney rolled her eyes and scoffed. "She laughed at me, saying if I was her competition, she wasn't the least bit worried. I tried to explain to her I'm not the girl she knew, that I'd grown, and I had ambition and talent. I'll be managing that store when it opens."

Apparently, Whitney's future reality hadn't kicked in.

Her eyes grew dazed, and she shook her head repeatedly. "But she just kept laughing. *Until tears came from her eyes.*" She exhaled and focused on me, her gaze now clear. "I don't know what happened after that."

The woman literally couldn't help herself, it seemed. "You don't know? Or you won't say?"

She folded her arms and stared into the distance. "I'd like to call an attorney."

Valerie and I shared a look before I answered. "That's probably for the best. I'm sure you'll be able to very soon."

Caden and two other police units arrived shortly after that. He rushed from his car and glanced between the three of us, assessing the situation. "I pointed to Whitney. She'd like to call her lawyer."

He arched his brow and then turned to Officer Brooke, who'd come up behind him. "Cuff her and read her rights. We're arresting her for the murder of Nan Collingsworth. Then let her make her phone call."

Brooke tossed her long blond braid over her shoulder and nodded, looking as stern as usual. "Yes, sir."

As his officer led Whitney away, Caden scanned the mess we'd created before turning to me with a look of incredulity. "Really?"

I shrugged and gave him a guilty smile. "Sorry. It seemed the safest way to get her to stop."

He folded his arms. "As opposed to allowing the police to do their job?"

Valerie raised her hand. "It's my fault. I got a little crazy there. I think Evie was just trying to manage the situation."

Caden shook his head in admonition. "Trust me. I heard everything you both said."

I pressed my lips together and gave him a smug nod. "I did my best."

He released a heavy sigh and turned to his crew. "Let's get this cleaned up and the cars off the road."

Then he faced us. "I'm taking you both to the station for statements. Someone will bring your car for you, Valerie."

She drew her brows. "There's nothing wrong with it, and I'm perfectly capable of driving."

He snorted as amusement flashed in his gray eyes. "I think you've done enough driving for today."

She tried to argue as he escorted us to his car and then switched to bribing him with cookies. I could have told her to give up, but I was suddenly too exhausted to care. I'd done what I could and my best friend was safe. That was all that mattered to me.

And sleep. I couldn't wait until I could take a nap.

EPILOGUE

I sat in my backyard, relaxing in a chair on the lawn, still wearing my frilly lavender maid-of-honor dress. Though I had grabbed a shawl before I'd headed outside to unwind for the day because it was slightly chilly.

Birdie, Kookie, and Momo were sprawled out on the grass near me, looking as content as I felt. Mochi was off harassing Gertie after Chloe's wedding, which was just fine with the rest of us.

"Chloe was stunning," Birdie murmured.

A happy smile curved my lips. "Yes, she was. She looked radiant. Her grandmother must have been a petite woman, too, because her dress fit Chloe perfectly."

My sweet familiar stopped licking her paw and looked at me. *What about me?*

I sucked in an impressed breath. "You, my little Kookie, were the most beautiful flower girl I've ever seen. Using your magic to toss the petals was a brilliant idea."

Her eyes sparkled with pleasure. *You helped.*

I gave her a small shrug. "Only a little."

Birdie crept through the grass until she was at Kookie's side. She pinned her daughter with a paw and began licking her ears. "Your magic is lovely, my sweet girl. Be proud of yourself."

I could tell from the look on Kookie's face she was thrilled.

The cats suddenly lifted their heads and glanced behind me. I turned to find Caden coming through the back gate, dressed in a hoodie and jeans. I cast him a sly glance. "You're out of your suit already."

He scratched the bottom of his neck and grinned. "They make me itch."

I held out my hand as he approached. "You'd better get used to it. You'll have to wear it most of the day at our wedding."

He chuckled as he wrapped his fingers around mine and crouched in the grass next to me. "Besides the bride, it looks like I have the three prettiest ladies at the wedding here with me."

Kookie purred, and my Aunt Birdie beamed. Little Momo seemed pleased, but I doubted she understood him other than to know he'd smiled at her.

Everything seemed perfect until the nasty little reminder popped into my mind, urging me to come clean with Caden. I needed to. The one thing solving Nan's murder had taught me was that being honest with people would make my life much easier.

And there was no time like the present.

I eased out a nervous breath and shifted toward him. "Caden, there's something I need to tell you."

He arched his brows, his expression pleasant and relaxed. "What's that?"

My stomach muscles tightened, and my survival instincts kicked into full gear, telling me to run instead. But I stayed strong. "This is going to sound really weird, but you've been with me long enough to know strange things happen in my life, right?"

He shrugged and nodded. "Don't worry about it. Just tell me."

I shifted my gaze to Birdie, who encouraged me with a nod. Then I blurted out my confession before I could change my mind. "My Aunt Birdie isn't dead. She's living in Theo's body with her."

Caden stared at me for a long moment, looking absolutely stunned. He placed a hand on his chest, and his eyes rolled as he toppled over in the grass.

My heart lurched in my throat, and I dropped to the ground next to him. I couldn't have shocked him that much, could I?

I took his face between my palms, looking for signs of distress before I patted his cheek. "Caden? *Caden? Wake up.*"

I was ready to call for emergency services when I noticed the corner of his mouth quirk. His eyes flew open, and he threw his arms around me, tugging me down to his chest as a laugh rumbled from inside him.

It took me a moment to speak. "Why are you laughing? Don't you believe me?"

His smile softened, and he drew a finger down my cheek. "Yes, I believe you."

I shook my head, bewildered. "But you don't seem surprised at all."

He rolled me from him and sat, pulling me up with him. "That's because I'm not."

I blinked several times. "Are you saying you already knew? How? When?"

"I found out not long ago." His gaze slid to Kookie. "When a mischievous little kitten paid me a visit."

I shifted my gaze to my familiar. "*You* told him?"

She gave me a firm nod. *You needed help.*

All kinds of thoughts popped into my head, and I wanted to berate her and explain it wasn't her story to tell. But... she'd done it out of love. I released a soft huff and turned to Birdie. "Did you help her?"

My aunt quickly shook her head. "I didn't say a word."

Caden jerked his gaze to my aunt, looking bewildered.

Kookie jutted out her chin. *I did it all on my own.*

"But how?"

She stood and strode close to me, rubbing her soft fur against my hand. *I just kept telling him until he understood.*

I turned my gaze to Caden. "Explain."

His eyes glittered with happiness. "I can't. Maybe she tapped into our connection. All I know is she showed up at my doorstep and mewed and mewed at me. Then

I felt a sliver of... knowing? I'm not sure. But I heard her right now telling you she figured out how to tell me on her own."

I was shocked. Stunned. Flabbergasted.

Birdie drew closer, regarding Caden with a hesitant gaze. "Hello there, young man."

A warm smile broke over his face, and he gathered my fluffy black and white cat aunt into his arms and hugged her. "Hello there, dear Birdie. Man, how I've missed you."

She chuckled. "Well, I was here all along, wasn't I?"

He laughed and set her on the grass. "I guess so. Still, it's good to have you back."

Birdie glanced at Momo, Kookie, and me. "I don't live alone anymore. I have a family now."

Tears sprang to my eyes. "All of us, Birdie. We're all your family."

We basked in our newfound happiness for a while before the kitties wandered off and the evening temps grew too cold to be outside. Caden helped me to my feet, and we walked to the house together. At the porch, he paused and narrowed his gaze at me. "No more lies or secrets between us, right?"

I gave him a happy smile and nodded. "No more. Only good things. Only love."

He pulled me into his arms and kissed me. "Good. Because that's all we need."

****

I hope you enjoyed the ninth book in the Cookie Corner Cozy Mystery series. Book 10, Bespelled Cookies is available for pre-order and will be released on March 5, 2024..

Sign up for my newsletter to receive notifications of new releases, freebies, and special sales at www.Cindy Stark.com

Also, if you have a moment, I'd appreciate a review!

Thank you very much, and happy reading,

Cindy

****

Keep reading for an excerpt from Mystic Murder, the prequel to the Mystic Village Mysteries. You can find the full novella for FREE as part of a ProlificWorks promotion at https://claims.prolificworks.com/gg/hG SP46zhOOWpPa5GW0

Excerpt: Mystic Murder

Mystic Village Mysteries

The spring morning in the high desert town of Mystic, Arizona, dawned bright and lovely. As I sat in the paved courtyard of the sandstone stucco home that I shared with a wise old witch named Mary Mae Martin, I sipped a warm cup of tea and basked in the thought that life couldn't be more perfect.

I had a safe and beautiful place to live, which hadn't always been the case. The trumpet flowers on the orange jubilee bushes were blooming, and I'd be opening my new gift shop very soon. I'd found a suitable space across from the picturesque outdoor shopping village where tourists loved to amble about, purchasing reminders of their stay in a town known for healing and many things paranormal. My shop would only be a short walk across the bridge with the pretty Willow River running beneath it, and I was counting on a portion of the people visiting the nearby stores to come over.

My lease started that day, and I was eager to get to my new Enchanted Elements shop. After breakfast, I planned to head over to make sure everything was ready for the shipments of books, crystals, and candles, among other things that would soon start arriving.

I'd lived through many uncertainties in life, but I'd planned this one so carefully that nothing could go wrong. I inhaled the scent of my cherry sencha tea as I sipped, closed my eyes, and smiled. Life was good.

The sound of the screen door screeching as it opened disturbed my serenity. It wasn't that Mary Mae or I couldn't fix the door, she simply wouldn't let me. She liked the squeak because she said she could hear people coming. Since Mary Mae was also psychic, that made no sense to me at all. But whatever. It was her house, and she could do what she wanted.

As she walked toward me, I lifted my gaze to the elderly woman, who was almost as round as she was tall. From what others had told me, Mary Mae had to be close to eighty, but she didn't look a day over sixty, and I wondered if she had a youth spell in her secret grimoire. "Would you like some tea? I brewed a full pot."

"Kalie."

The soft, compassionate tone of her voice was one I'd heard her use with others when she had bad news to deliver. I frowned and shook my head. "No."

I didn't know what bad news was coming my way, but I didn't want to hear it.

She strode closer and placed a comforting hand on my shoulder. The second she did, the phone buzzed in my pocket. I shook my head at her again, wishing that action would chase away whatever was about to transpire.

My heart sank as I glanced at my phone screen and recognized the name of the leasing company. "If I don't answer it, will they go away?"

Mary Mae gave me a sad smile, deepening the wrinkles around her dark brown eyes full of wisdom and compassion. "Sorry, child. It won't help you."

I steadied myself and answered the call. When the lending agent began by apologizing and then went into her spiel about how there'd been a mix-up, my head started spinning. But not enough that I didn't protest. "We have a signed contract, though. I have shipments coming in two days. You can't do this."

The woman released a deep sigh. "I'm sorry, Ms. Kennedy. Your insurance may cover the losses you'll incur until you can find a more suitable place. Check with them."

I huffed. "Can't I sue you and make you honor the contract?"

The woman cleared her throat. "I only facilitate the contracts. Your issue is with the owner. Whatever you choose to do is out of my hands."

She ended the call with another polite apology, and I stared at my phone as it reverted to the main screen. The tight knots in my stomach sickened me. "What am I going to do, Mary Mae?"

Her eyes twinkled. "Would you like me to consult the universe?"

By consultation, Mary Mae meant she'd look into her crystal ball. As it so happened, she was the most sought-after psychic in our little town, and rightfully so. Unfortunately, I'd discovered that her readings weren't always to my benefit and sometimes I preferred not to see what was coming. This time was different, though. Since my life had already taken a turn for the worse, it would be better to know now.

I gave her a cautious smile. "Do I have to pay?"

She chuckled. "You know the rules. One must give to receive."

I couldn't complain since she charged me a deeply discounted price, so I gave her a sheepish smile instead. "But I don't have a dollar on me. Can I add the amount to my rent?"

Mary Mae gave me a solemn nod. "You may. Come, child. Let's see what the universe has in mind."

When I stood, an uneasy feeling hit me, and it was strong enough that it knocked me back into my chair. I recognized that sensation as my intuition, and I'd learned the hard way to always listen. I didn't know what or why, but I knew I shouldn't go ahead with her reading. "Mary Mae?"

The old woman had her hand on the doorknob when she turned to me with questioning eyes. I released a shaky sigh. "Never mind. I think I'll handle this on my own."

She dipped her head in agreement. "Fair enough. I'll be inside."

My roommate returned to the house, leaving me alone with my fears. I sat, unmoving, for several moments, wallowing in the unfairness of the situation, until my conscience kicked me in the butt. Worrying would get me nowhere. I needed to take action.

So, of course, I called my best friend Jenna. She was one of the smartest women I knew, and even if she didn't have an answer, she usually led me in the right direction.

She picked up immediately, which hopefully meant she didn't have a full house at her coffee shop. "Hey, Kalie. What's up?"

"Oh, Jenna. I have a huge problem. Do you have a minute?"

Keyboard keys clacked in the background as she spoke. "Yeah. I'm in my office working on orders. Did you already lose the keys to your new shop?"

Emotion welled inside me. "I wish that was it. What I lost is my lease, and I have stuff being delivered the day after tomorrow. The agent said there'd been a mix-up, but I think someone probably offered to pay more than I was."

Jenna scoffed. "I told you that the people who own that building are shifty. But I think you might be in luck."

I was afraid if I breathed, I'd burst my new bubble of hope. "How so?"

"The Village's property manager was in this morning, and I overheard him talking about an available unit."

If there was, it would be a miracle. Mystic was a highly popular place where outdoor enthusiasts came to hike the beautiful red rock mesas and wounded souls came to heal. That meant retail space was difficult to find in my small town. "You're kidding. Where is it?"

"Give me a second to check the vendor's section on the website."

I pictured Jenna trying to tuck her dark hair that was too short to tuck behind her ear as she focused on her computer. "Believe it or not, it's inside Mystic Village and not the little strip mall he also manages. It is near the end of the outer courtyard where vendors don't get as much traffic. Could be why it's available."

I plastered my hand against my chest, unable to believe my good luck. "It's better than what I had. Oh goddess, Jenna. I have to talk to the manager now. I can't wait. Who do I call?"

Jenna blew out a breath. "Whoa. Slow down, Kalie."

I shook my head wildly. "I can't. Someone could be looking at it this instant. They might lease it by lunchtime."

My friend chuckled. "Okay. You're right. I'll call and see if the property manager can meet us there."

I hurried into the house to switch my sandals for sneakers. "Great. Tell him or her I'm headed there now."

"Shouldn't you wait to see if Mr. Bernard is available first?"

Waiting was not an option. The universe had given me a blessing, and I wasn't about to miss out on it. "No. If he's not, then I'll wait in front of the shop's door until he is. Text me what you find out."

It took me very little time to hop in my car and drive the few blocks to the picturesque collection of shops. Since it was still early, I found a close parking space and hurried from my car toward the red rock archway that was the hallmark of the shopping district.

As usual, passing through the archway left me feeling like I'd stepped into an alternate universe. Whoever had designed the sprawling shopping center had thumbed their nose at conventional architecture and design, preferring instead to give the charming place a wandering, vibrant atmosphere reminiscent of an old-time village in Mexico.

Three or four shops might be in a row, but then the cobblestone walkway would curve, leaving shoppers to meander through a maze of buildings in various shapes and sizes. Amidst it all, clay pots overflowed with colorful flowers. My favorites were the lime green sweet potato vines and cute yellow and pink lantana.

I rushed past several art galleries and the fudge shop until I reached the outer courtyard. From there, I strode along the pathway toward the river, peeking into any stores with darkened windows, until I spotted what appeared to be the vacant space.

Since many of the shops didn't open until later on the weekdays, I found myself alone. After my exertion, I filled my lungs to calm my breathing, smoothed my coppery auburn waves that had likely run wild from my exertion, and peered inside, as though I might find someone who'd beaten me there.

Except for a counter and fixtures that would be great for displaying my wares, the darkened store was empty. Someone had recently painted the outside trim and the door a pretty turquoise color, and a column of clematis rose from an aged whisky barrel filled with variegated ivy and pink geraniums.

It was perfect.

A message from Jenna popped up on my phone, telling me she and the property manager were on their way. And just like that, I was back to feeling good. Sometimes bad things led to better things, and that seemed to be the case for me.

I heard footsteps and lifted my gaze, expecting to see my best friend and the property manager, but when I found my nemesis, Sam Sullivan, walking my way, I frowned. The first day I'd arrived in Mystic, I'd been so enthralled by its red mesas and lush beauty that I'd accidentally bumped his car with mine. The light tap hadn't even left a scratch, but Sam had ranted on and on about me being an idiot.

Needless to say, we were not friends.

I thought he'd pass by with no interaction, but he stopped directly in front of me. I curled my lip to let him know I found his presence unpleasant. "What do you want?"

He snorted. "I want to know why you're standing in the doorway of my new shop."

I studied Sam Sullivan with his short blond hair, pretty hazel eyes, and faded jeans that fit him perfectly. I might have considered him handsome except for the viper's heart beating in his chest.

He claimed my new retail space belonged to him, but I knew for a fact that it didn't. Otherwise, the property manager wouldn't be on the way to meet me. So, I scoffed. "Good luck with that. This space is mine. I plan to sign the lease forms any minute now."

Sam glanced up and down the empty walkway. "Doesn't seem that way to me." He stepped closer, and I couldn't help but notice his powerful arms and the way he towered over me. "You should leave before you find yourself in trouble."

He didn't know it, but he didn't scare me in the least. A deranged witch hunter had almost killed me years earlier, and though they shared the same first name, this Sam didn't worry me a bit. That horrific experience had prompted me to learn as many protective spells as

I could, so even though Sam had nice muscles, he didn't frighten me.

Plus, I spotted a woman in the shop across the way peering out the window at us. "You'd better watch your step. What you said sounded like a threat to me, and just so you know, we're being watched. If you try anything, I'll call the cops, and I'll have a witness to back me up. I think it's best if you leave."

Sam huffed. "You're bluffing."

I planted my hands on my hips. "No, I'm being nice. If I wanted to, I could hex you on the spot and bring you to your knees. I'm one of those people you shouldn't mess with."

Instead of proving he was smart and walking away, he narrowed his eyes and stepped closer. "I guess it's up to me to call your bluff then, isn't it?"

I was a little on the short side, so I had to tilt my face upward to meet his gaze as I contemplated which spell would be the best. "Would you prefer excruciating leg cramps? Or maybe you'd like to black out? Except you might hit your head then, unless I was inclined to catch you. Which I'm not."

He folded his arms and regarded me with a sneer. "Oh, I see. You're a witch. Well then, you definitely won't want this place. It's haunted by a dark goblin that would love to prey on you and your powers."

I blinked, wondering if he was lying. If he wasn't, a malicious goblin would be a pain to deal with. But I'd been blessed with good friends like my mentor Tara and Mary Mae, who would help me with a powerful spell if needed. "Excruciating knee pain, it is."

I inhaled a deep breath. "Muscles and tendons, I summon—"

Unfortunately, Jenna called out before I could finish. "Hey Kalie. We're here."

Leave it to my best friend to show up and ruin the good part. I chuckled at Sam. "Lucky you."

Then I turned to Jenna, with her dark-haired, tapered bob and cat-eye glasses, before I glanced at the tall, slender man with a thick head of gray hair and waited for them to reach us. When they did, Jenna pursed her red lips and glanced between Sam and me. She ended by giving me a suspicious look, and I was certain she'd sense the powerful magic I'd left hanging in the air.

I shrugged my shoulders and gave her an innocent look before I focused on the property manager. "Hello. I'm Kalie Kennedy, and I'm extremely interested in this property."

The man glanced at Sam before he extended his hand and shook mine. "Chardon Bernard. Yes, the space is definitely available."

Excitement whipped through me. "Wonderful."

Sam stepped closer. "Char."

The property manager lifted a hand between them. "We'll talk later."

I was certain that was Sam's attempt to usurp me, but it didn't work. I smiled at Mr. Bernard. "My previous lease fell through, so I'd like to sign the one for this space today, if that's possible. I'm willing and able to put down a deposit. How much to lease it?"

Mr. Bernard drew a hand over this thick gray mustache. "What were you going to pay on your previous lease?"

I quoted the number and crossed my fingers that he'd agree to it.

The property manager curved his lips into a gratified smile. "We can actually go a little less than that."

I couldn't believe how much the fortunes were smiling on me that day. "Perfect. Can we look inside? It seems great from here, but I'd like to get a feel for the space. Honestly, I can't believe someone hasn't snatched it up already."

The man pulled out a set of keys and cleared his throat. "Of course, you can look around, but I must disclose that there's a reason it's still vacant. It's rumored to be haunted. Looking at statistics for the number of tenants that we've had during the past five years, it does appear there might be something that scares people away."

Dang it. Sam hadn't been lying. I shot Jenna a questioning look, and she responded by widening her eyes. I took that to mean that I shouldn't let anything chase me off until I knew exactly what I was dealing with. "Stuff like that doesn't really bother me."

Mr. Bernard unlocked the door and pushed it open for us. "Feel free to look around."

As we stepped inside, I flipped on the lights and linked my arm with Jenna's just in case a wicked goblin jumped out. The property manager stayed outside with Sam, which didn't ease my fears.

I squeezed Jenna's arm tighter as we walked toward the cash register that sat on a nearby counter. "Do you sense anything dangerous?" I whispered. "Sam said there's a dark goblin."

Jenna lifted her gaze as she slipped her arm from mine and surveyed the entire store. "No. Not that I can detect. You?"

I shook my head. "If it was something truly dark, we'd know, right? There should be an energy residue."

My friend nodded. "That's true. Though some of the craftier ones can hide it."

I drew my features into a nervous look. "If there really is a goblin, Tara and Mary Mae can help, don't you think?"

Jenna turned to me and curved her matte red lips into a smile. "Yes, I would definitely agree with that. We'd be doing you and poor Mr. Bernard a favor."

Her calm intelligence was one of the many reasons Jenna was my best friend. We balanced each other. She calmed my enthusiasm and what some called my feisty energy, which could get me in trouble. While she needed some chaos, meaning me, in her organized world.

I released a slow breath full of tension, feeling a hundred times more confident. Destiny had paved the way for me, and I shouldn't let anything hinder that. "Then

I'm going to go for it. Look at all the shelves and cases that are already here. The only thing I'll need to do is clean and stock the shelves. Honestly, it's much better than what the other place offered."

Jenna gave me a savvy nod. "It's meant to be. Hey, I need to get back, but once my afternoon manager shows up, I'll help with whatever you need."

I gave her a bright smile and hugged her. "This is all thanks to you. You're the best."

She winked at me. "I know. But I can't take all the credit. It's a new moon, and the perfect time to start a new adventure."

I walked her to the door, but we both stopped short when the two men's voices grew louder. Since Jenna and I had left the door open when we'd walked in, I had a clear view of Mr. Bernard, who'd drawn his brows in annoyance.

"You can't rent this out from under me, Char," Sam said, sounding angry. "We had an agreement."

It seemed I wasn't the only one Sam treated rudely.

Mr. Bernard heaved a deep sigh and shook his head. "No, we did not have an agreement. We had an understanding, and that was, if you came up with the deposit and first month's rent, I'd lease it to you. But if another vendor came along first, you'd be out of luck, and that's what happened."

Sam huffed. "I'm this close to selling a painting that will more than cover the cost. The buyer's extremely interested, and I'm just waiting for him to return to

Dale's shop. He said he would be in this week, so you need to give me a few more days."

Mr. Bernard shook his head. "I'm sorry, Sam. Keep saving your money. It's likely the place will be vacant in a month or two, anyway."

I frowned at what the property manager said while Sam cursed at the man and stomped away.

I slid a hesitant gaze to Jenna, as an uneasy sensation filled me. "It sounds like Mr. Bernard believes that whatever's here is going to scare us away."

She shook her head. "It might frighten some, but it's unlikely any of the previous occupants had access to the highly powerful women that you do. Can you imagine anything that would withstand Tara and Mary Mae?"

I pondered her question, thinking how lucky I was to have them in my life. "No. I've never come across anything that would stand a chance."

Jenna grinned. "Exactly. Now quit second-guessing everything. You'll be fine."

I blew out a deep breath. She was right. I'd never been good at having faith in things I couldn't control, but maybe it was time I learned.

We strode out together, and Jenna left us to return to work. I shifted my attention to Mr. Bernard. "The shop looks fantastic. Shall we sign the paperwork?"

He stroked his gray mustache and chuckled. "You really are raring to go."

I gave him an emphatic nod. "I most certainly am."

Mr. Bernard waved me forward and started walking. "Let's head to my office, then. Unfortunately, I can't finalize the lease today since it needs the owner's approval, but I can't see any reason it won't go through by tomorrow."

I supposed that would be fine. Waiting a day for a much better location would be worth it. After all, what could happen in twenty-four hours?

You can find the full novella for FREE as part of a ProlificWorks promotion at

https://claims.prolificworks.com/gg/hGSP46zhOOW pPa5GW0

Book List

COOKIE CORNER COZY MYSTERIES (PG-Rated Fun):

Cookie Calamity
Cursed Cookies
Killer Cookies
Enchanted Cookies
Secret Cookies

Haunted Cookies
Conjured Cookies
Shadow Cookies
Cookie Whispers
Bespelled Cookies

SWEET MOUNTAIN WITCHES COZY MYSTERIES (PG-Rated Fun):

Midlife or Death
One Midlife to Live
Midlife of the Party
Mysterious Midlife
Merry Midlife

For Once in My Midlife
Midlife in the Fast Lane
Such is Midlife
Love of my Midlife

CRYSTAL COVE COZY MYSTERIES (PG-Rated Fun):

Murder and Moonstones
Curses and Carnelian
Rumors and Rose Quartz

Brews and Bloodstone
Killer Kyanite
Hexes and Hematite

TEAS & TEMPTATIONS COZY MYSTERIES (PG-Rated Fun):

Once Wicked
Three Times Charmed
The Fifth Curse
Spellbound Seven
Nefarious Nine
A Witch Without a Spell

Twice Hexed
Four Warned
It's All Sixes
Elemental Eight
Hijacked Honeymoon
Mystical Mayhem

RETRIBUTION NOVELS (Sexy Romantic Suspense):
Branded   Hunted
Banished   Hijacked
Betrayed

BLACKWATER CANYON RANCH (Western Sexy Romance):
Caleb   Oliver
Justin   Piper
Jesse

ASPEN SERIES (Small Town Sexy Romance):
Wounded (Prequel)   Relentless
Lawless   Cowboys and Angels
Come Back To Me   Surrender
Reckless   Tempted
Crazy One More Time   I'm With You
Breathless

PINECONE VALLEY (Small Town Sexy Romance):
Love Me Again   Love Me Always

ARGENT SPRINGS (Small Town Sexy Romance):
Whispers   Secrets

OTHER TITLES:
Moonlight and Margaritas
Sweet Vengeance

ABOUT THE AUTHOR

Award-winning author Cindy Stark lives in a small town shadowed by the Rocky Mountains. She enjoys creating magical mayhem in her witch cozy mysteries, unexpected twists in her emotional romantic suspense, and forever love with hot guys in her sexy contemporary romance stories.

She'd like to think she's the boss of her three adorable and sassy cats, but deep down, she knows she's ruled by kitty overlords. Someday, she hopes to earn enough to open a cat sanctuary where she can save all the kitties and play all day with toe beans and murder mittens.

Connect with her online at:

http://www.CindyStark.com

http://facebook.com/CindyStark19

https://www.goodreads.com/author/show/5895446.Cindy_Stark

https://www.amazon.com/Cindy-Stark/e/B008FT394W

Made in United States
Troutdale, OR
11/03/2024

24389685R00119